Published by Under the Moon, LLC
Pelican Rapids, MN

Last Name
ISBN: 978-1-938339-42-4
Copyright © 2019 Terri Pray
Cover Art Copyright @ 2019 Samuel Pray
Editor in Chief: Terri Pray
All rights reserved.

Last Name

Terri Pray

Warning

This book contains sexually explicit scenes and adult language and may be considered offensive to some readers. Scars is for sale to adults ONLY, as defined by the laws of the country in which you made your purchase. Please store your books wisely, where they cannot be accessed by under-aged readers.

* * * * *

Last Name

Last Name is a novel set in the Tyme universe. Unless stated otherwise, all Tyme novels can be read as stand-alone titles.
Other Tyme titles.
Starfire https://www.amazon.com/dp/B01A7INM0E

Author's Note.

This book contains BDSM themes, and take down scenes. In fiction the trust required for this type of play can build in a matter of chapters. In real life please take care of yourself, and know who you play with. Have limits and a safe word in place before entering any BDSM scenes, no matter how well you believe you know your partner.

Keep it Safe, Sane, and Consensual. Or follow Risk Aware Consensual Kink.

Thank you.

Dedication

To my Sam.
Always.

Prologue

Corina arched her back and stretched out on the bed, careful not to disturb the sleeping figure next to her. She glanced down at the man, her fingers itching with the need to touch his dark, tousled hair to smooth the soft tendrils curled over the back of his neck. His toned body bare save for the corner of the sheet draped over the taut curves of his buttocks.

She licked her lips, remembering the feel of those same buttocks beneath her fingers as he'd pounded into her. The look in his eyes unmistakable with the way his pleasure had shone in their depths, as they'd both cried out only to collapse on the bed. It wouldn't take much to start all over again, but they'd done a decent job of wearing each other out in the past twenty-four hours, and he'd need his sleep.

And you don't?

Maybe she did, but she needed a shower first.

Her inner thighs ache, and she could feel the remains of the pleasures she'd shared with David. Not that she wanted to remove the reminder, but she had to. If she walked around smelling of sex, she'd never hear the end of it from the men and women she worked with, bad enough she was teased due to her mother's status as a Gaean Pleasure Adept.

With a sigh, she eased out of bed, naked as the day she'd been born, and padded across the room to her small bathroom.

The bathroom wasn't the largest on offer to those with private quarters, but it was better than the provisions on small ships, a few of the facilities had been tight enough you had to watch yourself if you turned too quickly, in case you ended up catching an elbow or knee on a corner. At least she did have it to herself unless she offered to let another woman share with her, or where the occupant had a lover.

Or husband.

Married. Her. Gods, it wasn't the type of thing she'd have ever expected. She knew how hard she was to get along with, and it had never been in her plans, but this man, this beautiful, strong, dangerous man had chosen her. He'd picked her, accepted her, and bonded with her using the Gaean ceremony in honor of her mother and the path Corina had turned her back on many years before.

Her mother. She'd have to contact Gaea and get a message to the Adept in the next couple of days. Not always an easy thing to do as her mother was one of the senior Adepts. Work which took her mother took her off world to one of the other five worlds, which were a part of system one. Although Gaea, Mars, Fate, Thanatos, and Chronos did not orbit the same star, they were known as system one due to the close ties between the worlds, and it wasn't uncommon for Adepts of one planet to visit or work with Adepts from another world.

Hells, what would the older woman say? It wasn't as if they'd spoken much in the past few years, but perhaps this would change her mind about the mistakes Corina had, apparently, made. Maybe they could find a level of peace at last.

She sighed and turned on the water, checking the temperature before stepping into the spray. *Luxury.* Yes, it was and one she'd never take for granted. Not after the year she'd spent on Mars, training with her father. Oh no, it had taught her such things as showers, hot water, and clean beds were luxury items which could be lost at any moment. She didn't regret the time spent on Mars in the training camp, but the lessons had been harsh ones with no room for mistake or weakness.

She scrubbed her fingers through her hair, washing the long reddish blonde strands. The soap was a plain one, she had no need for the seductive scents of her mother's calling or the oils the Adepts favored when they had a lover or a client. Still, the fact the soap produced thick, sensual suds was a bonus she wasn't about to turn down.

Corina smoothed handfuls of the thick liquid down over her breasts, cupping them as she washed. Her fingers found her still sensitive nipples and flicked them, causing a fresh shudder of pleasure to tingle through her body. Her inner walls clenched, a low need building between her thighs as she eased her hands down, washing carefully.

It would have been easy to slide her hand between her thighs and bring herself to...

"Room for one more?" His voice broke through her thoughts.

She dropped her hands and turned, smiling. "Always, husband." The triggered a new wave of warmth.

"Hmm, husband - I like the sound of that." David leaned against the doorframe, watching her for a moment longer. "Though I don't know if I want to give up the view."

"Then don't," she stretched, making sure he got an eyeful of her naked and wet form. "You could always stand and watch."

Oh, he could have stood and watched her for eternity, but he had only a few short hours before he had to leave. Fuck, this wasn't what he'd wanted or what he'd signed up for when he'd taken this mission. Then again, how could he have predicted finding a woman like Corina or falling for her?

Or marrying her.

If it hadn't been for the mission, he'd have been able to explore the idea of spending the rest of his life with her. Her combination of strength, intelligence, and sensuality was enough to draw any man's attention; he simply hadn't expected to be willing to go through with the marriage ceremony.

Was there a part of him that wanted more than the Shadow Rangers could offer?

Yeah, settle down? Me? So not happening. Not with a woman like this.

Yet the idea of leaving her left him feeling ill. Especially today.

But what choice did he have? He couldn't have turned her down, not when she'd asked him to marry her. A part of him which wanted to spend the rest of his life with her?

No, it's the drink. Enjoy the moment, give her a time to remember, then get out. Get out before it's too late.

"Have you made your decision yet?" She rested one hand on a cocked hip and smiled. "Or should I find another to keep me company?"

He growled under his breath and stalked toward her. "I don't think it would be a wise idea, love."

"Hmm, are you certain? After all, I don't want to get lonely in here," she turned slowly, exposing the tight, sensual curve of her back and ass. "And I don't want to take up your precious time."

Oh, she's asking for it. And he was all too ready to give it to her. He reached out, tangling his fingers in her hair. "Keep it up, and I'll have to bring you back to heel." He growled against her neck as he used the grip to pull her close.

"You don't have it in you." She laughed, struggling lightly in his grasp.

"Let's see about that." His grip tightened, and his cock throbbed at her soft cry. The soft play of the water from the shower added to his growing arousal. Each new touch teased and pulled at his cock, or dripped down from the head, down his shaft, to then tug free from his heavy sac. "It's time to put you to the test. Put your hands against the wall, now."

Corina purred and did as he ordered, her back arched tightly, her backside pressed out toward him. "And what do you have in mind, lover?"

More than we have time for. "You. Me. This wall." His words guttural.

"And if I object?"

He used the grip in her hair to turn her head slightly, enough to allow him to see into her eyes. "This." He brought his free hand against her backside with a loud crack.

"Ah." She cried out, a soft rock playing through her hips. "Naughty…"

"Yes, you are." He cupped her ass cheek before lifting his hand away and planting a second firm slap. "And I think it's past time I corrected your behavior."

Corina shuddered, her eyes closing, lips parting in a soft O.

"Thought so, you like it, don't you, Corina." He rubbed the heat of the smacks into her buttocks. "More?"

"Yes," she hissed.

He leaned in, grazing his teeth over the back of her neck, the head of his cock pressing against her backside. It wouldn't take much to slide between her thighs and fill her afresh.

Soon.

Yes, it had to be soon. They were running out of time.

"Beg me."

"More, David. Please, more." She purred, her eyes half opening, lips full, parted and kissable. "I want more, please."

"Want or need?" He bit down lightly, then traced the tip of his tongue over the bite. "Tell me the truth."

"Need," she growled, her hips rolling, rocking with an undeniable hunger. "Definitely need."

A declaration he wasn't going to argue with. He smiled and gave her what they both needed. First one slap, then another, ten more followed, each accompanied by a heated cry and a deep roll of hips. The water from the shower traced patterns down her back, sliding over the warmed skin and tempting him to simply take her.

"Now, please. Gods, now. I can't wait. I don't want to wait." She arched her back and pushed back against him. "Fuck me."

He shifted his weight, pressing the head of his cock between her thighs until her slick lower lips parted over the head of his cock. He released her hair and took hold of her by the waist before his hips moved.

The slick, tight heat of her sex wrapped and clenched around his cock and he bit back a groan. It would have been easy to lose control and slam into her, over and over again until he filled her. His fingers tightened as he rocked, slowly, sliding in and out of her heated core.

"Faster," she groaned, rolling her hips, tipping them, pressing back to meet his thrusts.

"Not yet," he was enjoying this too much.

"Yes," she pushed back from the wall enough to free one hand, then reached under, cupping his balls, stroking them. "Faster."

"Wicked wench." His balls tightened, threatening to spill before he was ready. Her touch, light, and teasing, enough to torment him to the edge of his sanity. "You're going to push me too far one day."

"Not today." She circled her hips, tipping them before pushing back to meet his next thrust. "Please, I don't want slow and loving. Not this time."

How could he ignore her plea?

He shifted his grip to her hips, holding her tight. His buttocks tightened, thighs clenched as he thrust into her without holding back. She whimpered, moving her hand back to the wall and bracing herself.

Each new thrust brought the slap of his balls against her slick, swollen flesh as he blinked water from his eyes.

Heat, pleasure, pressure, the slick rub, clenching muscles and mingled cries, all combined to push him close to the edge of sanity. He had to hold. Let her catch up. Let her find a moment of bliss before he…

"I-I can't hold any longer." She sobbed, moving with him.

"Then don't."

His balls tightened against the base of his cock, pain mingling with pleasure, his teeth clenched, jaw tight at the moment before it tore through him. His cock pulsed, his seed coating her inner walls and for a moment they stood, shuddering under the soft caress of the warm water.

His knees weakened, and he moved his hands to use the wall as a resting point. With his hands on either side of hers, and his lips pressed against her neck, he smiled, catching his breath.

"Gaea must have been smiling my way when you walked into my life," Corina murmured and shifted her weight. "And I'm going to have to light a candle the next time I'm near a temple."

He nibbled her neck and slowly moved free of her welcoming heat, doing his best to hide the tightness wrapped itself around his heart. She wouldn't feel this way about him tomorrow when she woke to find him gone.

But he was duty bound to leave, and she'd get over it. A woman like Corina wouldn't be long without a lover, and she'd find one better than him. A man willing to spend the rest of his life with her who would wipe all memories of his existence from her mind and she'd be better off without him.

"I love you," she turned to face him, wrapping her arms around his neck.

Silently David lifted Corina into his arms and carried her, still wet, out of the shower and back into the bedroom. If nothing else, he could watch her fall asleep in his arms before he crept out. With luck, she wouldn't wake until he'd been gone for a couple of hours.

And if she woke, he'd find a way to deal with that to.

This was simply how it had to be.

Chapter One

Pain exploded across her left cheek, the force of the blow enough to send Corina stumbling back against the bar. Breath left her body in a gasp as she pushed away from the hard edge behind her back and stepped left, ducking at the same time. The second punch flashed past her left shoulder, her attacker nothing more than a blur of beige tunic and massive fists to Corina's dazed vision.

Don't think, react. Deal with the pain later.

Easier said than done in a situation like this.

Glass shattered. A deep grunt followed by a high-pitched howl warned her of the danger to come. Scrambling, chairs scraping, footsteps, the sounds merged one barely distinguishable from the other. All except one, a voice which pierced the cacophony.

"Peacekeeper bitch, come back here. Not finished with you yet."

Fuck, did he think she'd be dumb enough to obey him? *Duh, obviously he does.* Corina shook her head, trying to clear her vision. Her right hand hovered over the butt of her gun, ready to palm it. She spat, clearing her mouth of blood and – shit – was that a tooth? She peered down at the small piece of white amid the red. Yep. The bastard had cost her a tooth.

She'd reclaim the payment for it out of his damned hide.

Corina dropped and rolled, coming up to her feet to the right and several feet away from the brute as she turned to face him again. Her weight shifted onto the balls of her feet, her knees flexed, gaze fixed on her target.

"Lieutenant Greenheart, do we need any backup?" Her partner called out but kept a safe distance from the fight at least for now.

He's keeping back out of the way. I don't need the distraction of another body in the middle of this.

"No. Stay where you are." Corina didn't glance back toward the source of the voice. Fuck, her jaw hurt. First stop after dealing with idiot boy here would be medical. Fortunately, such visits were covered by work, or they'd make a hell of a dent in her credit. "Hert, if you make me draw my gun you'll end the day in the morgue instead of the tank."

"Funny little peacekeeper bitch, aren't you. Think a scrawny thing like you can take me down? Think you can beat me?" Hert Tumle looked down at her, his three golden eyes fixed on her. At nearly eight feet tall and a grey cast to his skin, Hert was a formidable opponent unless you knew how to handle his kind. "Already knocked you down once, haven't I? Do I need to do it again before you get the message? Stupid female should know better by now. Might be I need to teach you a lesson or four. Maybe I take you before I send you to peacekeeper morgue."

Sure, fine, at five foot nothing she had a small disadvantage when faced with an eight-foot walking wall. Yeah, she knew what he was thinking. They all made the same mistake when it came to a fight with her. They judged her by her size, or worse, size and gender, their loss, her gain. Tomolins were an arrogant species with no use for females outside of the breeding pits. They kept their off-world dealings to males wherever possible, and those rare members of their species who tried to be diplomatic had an issue hiding their contempt for females. Add alcohol into the mix, and all bets were off. Worse, they had one weakness in a fist fight; a single spot on the right-hand side, between the upper and lower rib cages.

Yeah, all she had to do was find a way to that spot and hit it with everything she had, and Hert would be flat on his back with his eyes rolled up, whimpering for his mom — or whatever Tomolins cried out for when they were hurt.

I hit him, and he goes down. Real simple, right?

"Come here female, and maybe I'll show you the best use for one like you." His face split into a grin, a rumbling laugh from a dozen of the males in the bar, echoed through the room. "Maybe I give you to them when you've learned your place, little female?" He was losing control of his use of basic, switching to the more guttural language which was indicative of his kind. "Think you like the idea. Think it is why you come after me. Yes? I know your type. Need male to show you your place."

Mensarians, yeah, the laugh had to be from their side of the bar. Typical. Tomolins and Mensarians in the same damn bar. Made her fucking day. The Mensarians attitude toward females matched – in many respects – that of the Tomolins and they'd been at war with their sister planet – where males were kept subjugated – since the early days of space flight.

What else could go wrong? Maybe a group of slavers walking in at the same time? If the timing was right, they'd show up any minute now...

No slavers?

Oh well, she couldn't have it all.

"Are you finished with the bad boy speeches? Or did you plan on boring me to death? You're already repeating yourself, you know. But I shouldn't be surprised considering the limited size of your --- mind." Corina took care to drawl out the words.

Alarms droned outside of the bar. Someone cried out, a scuffle erupting behind her but she didn't turn. The noise grew with each passing heartbeat, but she couldn't spare the time, not unless she wanted to lose her life in the process.

Fuck, I don't need this.

But maybe she could use it.

Hert's gaze flickered to the source of the fight. His weight shifted left for a moment and a moment was all she needed. Corina slipped her hand to the belt cinched about her waist, grabbing the set of illegal brass knuckles she hid deep in her pocket and slipped them one. In one swift move, she darted forward, ducking under his reach before he'd settled his gaze upon her again, and slammed her fist into his exposed side, right into the gap between the upper and lower cages.

The Tomolin grunted, blinking slowly as he stared down at her, but Corina had already moved, darting back away from him and his immediate reach. He coughed, his eyes watering as he took a single step forward.

Shit, don't let him be one of those damn bastards that can push past...

Hert shook his head, taking another step toward her.

She slipped the knuckles back out of sight. If he spotted them, if he realized what she'd used to strike him, it would only make matters worse. Weapons like the knuckles were against the rules for a peacekeeper, but she'd never been one to follow the rules.

They were more like guidelines anyway.

"Bitch." He hissed the word out.

"Yeah, you said that already." It hadn't worked. She'd missed the spot. Any minute now he was coming after her, and all hell was going to break loose. If she were lucky, then she'd wake up in medical, if not...

Hert's heavy body dropped to his knees, then slowly, painfully, he crumpled to the floor.

Which is when the shit hit the fan.

"You're lucky you didn't break anything, Corina." Chief Medical Officer Piotr Astra shook his head and set the tray aside an hour later, his intense violet eyes and gold dusted skin marked him as a Valkyrie, but unlike most of his race, he'd chosen the path of a healer instead of a warrior. "And don't bother telling me there was no other way, I've already seen the report in all its glorious detail. Amusing in its own way, especially the bit about the brass knuckles – oh, don't worry it wasn't in the report, but it wasn't hard to figure out if you knew what to keep an eye out for."

Corina's jaw tightened, but she bit back a reply. The last thing she needed was a fight with one of the few men on the station who respected the uniform she wore. It wouldn't have been too bad if she hadn't been the daughter of a Gaean Pleasure Adept, but she was, and there was no hiding the *gifts* her bloodline had left her with. Piotr, however, had never judged her for her appearance or how she moved. Instead, he'd waited, taken the time to get to know her and as such the respect which had formed between them was a bond she would always be grateful for.

The brass knuckles, if she were caught with them, would add more complications to an already nasty situation. That might be the excuse Kraven might be looking for to be rid of her once and for all. "Bringing it back up would have made things ten times worse, Piotr. They were itching for a fight, and this way I kept the casualties down to a reasonable level."

The Valhallian male turned the full force of his violet gaze on Corina. "Try telling it to a man who doesn't know you, my friend. You're always ready for a fight. Most of the time you keep it under control, but you've been itching for a knockdown for the last thirty days or more. I've noticed the amount of time you've logged in at the gym. Don't try and fool yourself or me."

"Okay, fine, if I'd called them in at the beginning then maybe the bar would still be in one piece. But I wouldn't place any bets." Corina rubbed her aching temples, trying to chase away the pounding pain throbbed through her head. Okay, he was right in every way possible. She had wanted a fight. One which would ease the turmoil in her soul and settle her fraying nerves, but she hadn't gone in determined to destroy the bar. *No, it was a fringe benefit.* "Hert wasn't about to back down, if you'd taken a read through his record you'd know, Piotr. The male's in question is a complete asshole."

Every member of the service on the station knew about him.

The healer sat on the edge of the bed, folding his hands in his lap. Despite his warrior background, Piotr was a gentle male who found peace in his calling as a healer, but it did nothing to lessen his strength. A strength he now used when he addressed her.

"Corina, I'm aware of his record. I've dealt with him, or rather his victims, before. But you're trained to handle these situations, you know better than to charge in the way you did."

She opened her mouth to interrupt.

"No, listen to me, please." He lifted his hand, cutting off her words with a curt gesture. "Don't forget my people are warriors, just as your father's people are. The training remains with me to this day despite the path I have dedicated myself to." He sighed and closed his eyes for a moment, his jaw tight before it eased, and he fixed his gaze upon her once more. "My sister was the chosen of her age, and yet where did it lead her? The woman who should have been the shining light of our era and now she's an outcast. Though she saved our people, stopped a war, she broke the rules, and is now exiled from our world."

"And your point is?" Valk's were a law unto themselves anyway. They might be related to her father's people, but the bloodlines had parted ways during the dawn of space travel – or long before if the legends were to be believed. Sure she knew more of the story than anyone else did outside of the Valk homeworld, but this was different. She hadn't broken the ultimate laws of her home, either home. In fact, she'd held to them through every struggle she had ever faced.

Piotr's jaw clenched.

Okay, bad move.

"Yes, I know, she's your sister. She's family. What's it got to do with how I handle things?" Different rules, different situations, the Valk's weren't exactly forgiving when it came to traditions. She smiled, her own people weren't so different, or at least her father's people.

Her mother's, they were a different matter, but they held their own traditions sacred. She hadn't sworn to either the path of a healer or a pleasure adept, nor would she ever. Shit, she didn't have the instincts for healing, let alone the Psionic gifts which could make much easier to deal with. As for the pleasure side of things, she preferred to keep those private and not offer them to those coming to the temples in search of help or a moment of sexual healing.

The man flicked his violet gaze up, shook his head, and took a deep breath before he glanced at her again. "She's like you, in many ways. Astaria, she acts without thought of leaning on others around her, when she's been trained to do otherwise. She could have put an end to all of this if she'd asked for help from the right people. But no, she was too proud, and by the time she realized how deep she was in, it was too late. She did what she needed and was cast out. An outlaw and a heroine all rolled into one, yet I know she'd give up the heroine part if she could step foot on Valhalla one more time."

Corina closed her eyes and sighed. "Fine, maybe I should have called people in before I walked into the bar. But I survived, and the fight that followed, well it was the Mensarians idea of fun." And the fact those men had been there should have told her she was walking into trouble. Shit, she knew better. "I won't do it again. Okay, I'll try not to do it again. If I feel the urge to dive headfirst into chaos, I'll come and talk to you if possible."

Piotr didn't respond.

"I was in the wrong. I acted without thinking, and I'm sorry, 'kay?" He had his way, she'd said it. It was over and done with. What more could he want from her?

"It's not me you need to apologize to, Corina, and I'm sure the Captain will have a few sharp words for you, once he's picked up the pieces." Piotr filled in a few details on the datapad he carried.

Captain Kraven, wonderful, she'd all but forgotten about him.

Yes, she'd have to face the man, get the dressing down out of the way and try and talk herself out of the ultimate punishment of being released from duty. Gods, if her father still lived, he'd come hunting for her if she was removed from her duty post, the dishonor would have been more than he would have been willing to put up with. "Shit, and he's either on his way here or sent word to you that I'm to report to his office, right?"

"I expected him here half an hour ago." Piotr glanced at the clock on the wall. "I'm guessing a more important matter came up, and he expects you to go to his quarters."

"Fine," she sat up on the edge of the bed. "Am I cleared?" *Please say yes. I'll behave for the rest of the day if you say yes.*

"For duty, no. To leave Medical, yes." Piotr shook his head. "Though I'd prefer it if you stayed here until he arrived. At least that way I'll know what's going on."

"I'd prefer not to have an audience for the reaming out he's going to give me, Piotr. Thanks, though." She flashed a smile and stood up, glancing toward the door. "Besides, once the Mensarians get word to their people about the beating they took, there'll be more than a few reprisals. And you know what it means; we're both going to be swamped with work."

If they were lucky, there'd only be a few injuries. If not... it wouldn't be the first time the Mensarians had taken advantage of a situation or used it as an excuse.

The older man nodded slightly. "In that case, you'll be back here before the end of the night either under my care or as an escort. I'll be informing Kraven about my decision, don't think you can find a way to avoid it."

She wasn't going to argue. With a smile, she headed for the door. Kraven would be in his office, and once the fight – er – reaming was over and done with, she could return to work. He wasn't in a position to put her on light duties or remove her from active service.

Not unless I've pissed him off and taking me off duty will help smooth things over with the owner of the bar?

It wasn't exactly all her fault. She hadn't counted on the men in the bar. Shit, she hadn't fired at them. She'd not said a word to them. They hadn't been her problem. Unfortunately, at least one of the men in the crowd knew her. Which was all they needed to turn the group of men against her, and the fight, the destruction of the bar, had been inevitable.

Kraven, he was a fair man, but he was still the Captain, and he had the right to suspend her for not following protocol. She'd stepped out of line, at least as far as the rules were concerned, he'd deal with her. But had she done enough to be removed from duty permanently? She didn't think so, and if she had then perhaps, she would be able to talk her way out of it. Then the matter would be over and done with. Okay, if she had to stand down for a day or so, she could handle it. Hell, she could do with the rest after everything which had happened.

Corina stood in front of the door to his office and took a deep breath. She tapped, lightly, on the door and waited for a sound. It came, nothing more than a murmur, but a voice she recognized. With a calm smile fixed in place, she walked into Captain Kraven Kallinski's office and stopped, her jaw instantly tightening, her gaze locking with a man she hadn't expected to see, nor had she wanted to ever see again.

"Corina…"

Chapter Two

Shit, this isn't exactly going to go as I planned. David Monroe stood up and met Corina's gaze. This wasn't what he'd had in mind when he'd agreed to meet Kraven for a drink. Shit, he hadn't known Corina had been on the station until he'd caught sight of the young woman during the mess at the end of the bar fight.

Had he misjudged the time that badly? He hadn't believed it possible and had tried to give plenty of time before arriving with a bottle in hand for Kraven. It had been a damn good bottle as well and now sat, still unopened, on the desk in front of Kraven.

Damn waste.

"Perhaps we should have a drink another time, Kraven?" He didn't look at his old friend, no matter how much he wanted to tear his gaze away from Corina.

She'd changed, and for the better. Corina stood with her head held high, despite the fact she obviously didn't want to be there. Short reddish-blonde hair, semi-curled at the ends, barely brushed across her shoulders instead of the near waist length hair she'd had when they'd first met. Her lush lips parted for a moment, then clamped shut, forced into a tight, thin line. His gaze traced slowly down the length of her body, taking in the taut lines of her well-toned body. Then he made the mistake of letting his gaze linger on her chest. Her full breasts strained at the uniform she wore, giving a hint to the lush body which lay waiting for the right man to touch.

Waiting for me and only me.

What else did he expect? How would he react if another man tried to touch them, touch her, in front of him? No matter what had happened in the three years since they had last seen each other, she remained his wife. No divorce filed, nothing save the fact she was married on the quick record he'd been able to pull up since he'd spotted her at the end of the bar fight; nothing which included a mention of who she was married to.

Why the hell hadn't she listed him as her husband?

Was there another in her life now? Fuck, if she'd taken a lover, how would he react?

Death, destruction, mayhem, blood coating the walls, floor, and ceiling. Maybe a few screaming civilians in the background or a dead body or three?

He shook his head and chased the idea away. Their time was over and done with, and it was better that way. He'd walked away from her, followed through with the orders he'd been given and never glanced back. Never allowed himself to peer into the past. Until now.

Should never have left her. Screw orders, I married her. Should have fucking stayed with her. It would have been the right thing to do.

But he hadn't. He'd clung to the order, left and hadn't contacted her for over a year after they'd parted ways. She hadn't been happy about the contact. Death, dismemberment and other threats had followed during their brief contact via long distance com. He hadn't tried again and had done his best to push all memory of Corina to the back of his mind.

Now she stood before him, every inch the beautiful, sensual woman he remembered.

It would be better for both of them in the long run if he never thought of her again. Better for his sanity and his physical health because damn if he tried to touch her again she'd have the right to rip out his guts and feed them to him.

She might manage it. Gods alone know she beat me a time or two in our matches.

He understood all the danger and temptation she presented. He knew keeping his distance was the only sane move he could make. Then why did his cock still harden at the sight of her? Not harden but throb, ache, pulse with the need to part her thighs and bury himself deep in her body. He took a deep breath, trying to bring his desires under control, but it didn't work.

Toast. Complete and utter toast. Well done – no, screw that – burned. And it's my own fucking fault.

"No, stay David. This won't take long, and I believe you witnessed at least some of the altercation in question." Kraven's gaze rested on David for a moment before he turned his attention on Corina. "Lieutenant. Greenheart, do you have a problem with following the regulations?" Kraven's cold, calm voice filled the room.

Her gaze focused on Kraven, dismissing David's presence without a word. "No, Captain."

"Then explain to me exactly what happened on level five." Kraven leaned back in his chair, never moving from behind his desk. "Why didn't you call in for back up when you realized the Mensarians were present? You know the rules, Lieutenant. Male peacekeepers call in if we're dealing with Mensans, females if to work with the Mensarians. It's the best way to handle the situation, always has been and always will be. You're not going to be able to change their views on opposite genders. The war has been going on for longer than either of them are capable of recalling and it's unlikely it will end any time before the energy death of the universe."

Ah yes, the infamous gender war between the twin planets of the system. Not a matter any sane man or woman would ever want to get into the middle of. The reason Freedom Station had been built had been to prevent the war from spilling out across the stars or the two worlds annihilating each other. He'd been fortunate enough to stay clear of any of the problems caused by the twin worlds on his previous visits to the station. If things went according to plan, he'd continue to keep out of it.

He'd known of more than one member of the Shadow Rangers who'd been sent into a mess for one reason or another. Not him. Never him. Shit, he'd resign first.

"I didn't have time before the wrath of Mars was unleashed,

sir," Corina replied her voice calm – at least to anyone who didn't know her.

"Bullshit. You had the fuckin' time, Lt. The minute you walked in, you had to have known those men were present." His voice pitched low and steady. "Don't try and fool me, Lieutenant. Been there. Done it. Got the damn T-shirt. You can't pull that shit past me."

David sat still, taking care not to draw attention to himself as he listened to the exchange. This wasn't his fight, and he wasn't about to give either opponent the chance to pull him into this.

Corina's stance barely changed, nothing more than a flicker of darkness across her face, a stiffness about her shoulders as they slumped fractionally, then came back up. "Things moved quickly once I entered the bar, sir. I didn't have time to fully assess the situation or double check who was in the bar. I focused on the suspect."

"You expect me to buy that one when you stopped your partner from calling for back up?"

Tiny lines tightened around Corina's eyes. "No sir, I mean yes, sir I stopped my partner from calling for back up."

"You had time to think about your actions."

"Yes, sir." Her gaze never flickered from Kraven's face. "I did."

"And now you've had time to think the situation through?" Kraven moved his left hand to a datapad. "What would you say about your decision now?"

"I acted foolishly, sir." Her chin lifted a further. "I made a mistake which could have proven fatal for myself and my partner. I endangered the lives of the bar patrons in the process. In short, I would have better served the station and my partner by allowing the call for back up to be made."

"And?" Kraven arched an eyebrow.

"I can't say it won't happen again, sir."

"Why is that? I want the truth, Lieutenant."

David frowned but said nothing. He had no idea why Kraven

was pushing things, but he had to believe the man knew what he was doing.

"The whole truth, sir. All right. We both know saying such might be a lie. I have shown, before now, I don't always make the best choices. However, in my defense, I'll also state that, normally, my gut instinct is right. Even when I've acted in haste, I haven't lost a partner, or seen a civilian injured once I've taken control of the situation." She took a deep breath, pausing for a moment before continuing, and when she did her voice remained calm and clear. Controlled. "With that in mind, I would understand if you decide you need to relieve me from duty. I broke protocol, and we still don't know what will happen if the Mensarian embassy decides to get involved in the aftermath. They tend to be dogmatic about such things, and it would force you into a position where you would have to act regardless of any personal beliefs. Not that I'm saying you'd ever let your personal beliefs get in the way of things and – and I'm shutting up now." She forced her shoulders back more, her gaze focused on Kraven as she waited on his decision.

One thing she'd never lacked for was courage, no matter if it was misplaced at times. She'd grown since they'd last met and her courage was a facet he'd missed. He'd seen her display her fearlessness more than once but seeing it again brought it home for him. He wasn't sure he'd have the courage to stand up to the man who was his commanding officer at least not in such a blatant manner at least.

"You're relieved of duty for the next twenty-four hours. Is that understood?"

Her gaze narrowed, anger flaring across her eyes. "Yes, sir." Her words clipped and short. "I understand."

"Step over the line in any form, and you'll be suspended for an extra day. Push me, and you'll be out of here. I'll have you shipped out before you have time to figure out what's going on. Now, get out of here. I don't want to see you here, or in uniform, until this time tomorrow."

She nodded once, turned and left the room without another word, and only as she turned to leave, did her gaze flicker in David's direction. Heat flushed across her cheeks before she fled the room, and David was all too aware he was the cause of the blush.

Was it because he was here and had witnessed her dressing down or because of memories of the times they shared together? He couldn't ask her in front of Kraven. He glanced at the bottle, then back at the door. No bottle of booze was worth giving up the chance to talk to Corina.

"Interesting," he murmured, then looked back at Kraven who had already poured himself a drink, which he downed in one swallow, "but I'm not sure she appreciated me being here. Especially not with our history." His fingers itched with the need to touch Corina again, and if he didn't do give in to the demand, it would burn him up from the inside out. "I should go before she comes back to have a more private word with you."

"She won't, and you know it, which means you have another plan else in mind. Don't try and deny it, it's a waste of time for both of us." He frowned and met David's gaze, draining the glass a second time.

"I don't know what you mean…"

"HeHYou mean to hunt Corina down and try to talk to her. Pin her against a wall and force her to see you."

"Maybe." Damn a drink appeal to him right now, but if he was going to follow Corina, he'd need a clear head.

"It's your funeral. You know how's she's likely to react to you trying to push things, don't you? She'll react. Violently. Yeah, okay, no point in trying to persuade either of you, I know that. The way you two act anyone would think it had been more than a passing fling between you." Kraven shook his head, then grinned before he turned his attention toward the now closed door. "She'll be heading for the gym if I know her. She'll need to burn off steam before it finds another, more dangerous way to be released. She won't want to get into more trouble, but if she doesn't let it out somewhere, it will burn her up from the inside."

Had there been more than a few weeks of shared pleasure between them? David frowned wondering what Kraven was seeing that he was missing.

Yes. Mine. Always mine.

Except she wasn't. The relationship had helped with his cover. It had been the right thing to do. Leaving had been a case of following orders.

Sure. Yeah. Whatever.

"If you want to head her off before she hits the gym, you'll need to go now."

Yeah, of course, the gym. Where else would she go when she was pissed off? She'd need a target to beat up, a punch bag maybe? When they'd first met, she'd been angry and had beaten the hell out of a body-sized punch bag.

"Fuck," Corina swore, her hands clenched at her sides as she stormed down the corridor. He shouldn't have been on the station. Worse, David Monroe should have been anywhere but Kraven's office. He didn't work for the station. He wasn't in the peacekeepers. He shouldn't have been allowed to sit and observe while Kraven dressed her down.

What the hell was he doing on the station in the first place? David should have been on the other side of the universe, or better yet locked up in jail. He had no right to turn up here. This was her place. Her home. Her work. Not his.

He had no right to be there when Kraven was dressing her down, she couldn't get past that part. The idea of him sitting, listening, watching the entire thing, left her fuming. He wasn't a part of the service. A damn visitor to the station and yet Kraven had embarrassed her by forcing the situation. A matter David, no doubt, had enjoyed every damned minute of.

He's fucking lucky I didn't kill him.

He had no right to be here. This was her damn place, and he should have turned around, left the moment he'd realized she was here.

And which rules of the station forbid an ex from turning up? I must have missed that rule in the book.

Okay, he had a right, but he should have found a way to contact her. Warned her and she could absent herself or find a way to keep herself busy. He must have known she was on the station. A man like him always checked anything of importance before docking.

Right, as if he was supposed to give me notice in case I wasn't ready to see him. It's not as if I am important to him. He left me.

He couldn't have known she was here, could he? No, of course not. He wouldn't have checked the duty roster for her or anyone else. He wasn't the type to track her down and turn up to give her grief. She'd been nothing more than a quick fuck. Okay, not a quick one; a repeat fuck he'd lost interest in when she was no longer convenient for him. This was a coincidence, nothing more, nothing less.

The knowledge didn't change how she felt, either about the man, or the situation. The lies, all those damnable lies, and worst of all had been the one about his name.

Perhaps there had been a reason for the lie? One he couldn't tell me about.

No, she couldn't think that way, not after the way he'd left her. No note. Would it have killed him to let her know where he'd gone?

He did let me know what had happened, sort of.

It didn't count as it was months after the fact. Long after the wound through her soul had been left to go septic, and her heart turned to ice. Ice which had threatened to melt at the first fresh glimpse of his rugged features. Only then had he contacted her through a third party and given her his real name or the name he claimed was genuine.

Monroe.

His excuse. He'd had orders to leave. He hadn't said from whom. Nor had he worked for the Peacekeepers, or any other agency she'd known of. Had he meant a client? He'd refused to go into details and instead left her with a new wave of pain and grief. She'd meant so little to him he hadn't tried to tell her in person. Sure, okay, he'd given the excuse of work but what the hell was important about being an Indie Captain, and why did it mean he couldn't stop and talk to her?

He's never told me the entire truth about who he is and what he does.

Now he was in the station, and she had to deal with him.

I don't want to deal with him. I never want to deal with him again. Son of a bitch shouldn't be here. This isn't his place, to begin with. It's mine. I'm safe here. Or – or at least I should be.

Damn him, he hadn't changed. His body, his eyes, the way he moved, and the steel wrapped in velvet tone of his voice, they all called to her in a way she couldn't fight. No, the best thing for her was to put as much distance between them as possible and pray for the day he left the station.

She didn't want to deal with him. He was too dangerous – at least as far as her heart was concerned. He'd hurt her far more than anyone should have the power to do and now he was back in her life, ready and willing to dig his way into her heart and mind once more.

He won't be here long.

For all she knew he was already on his way to a ship which would take him to another sector. Why if she wanted him out of her life did the idea of him leaving without speaking to her make her feel sick?

She didn't want to talk to him, did she?

Not only no, but hell no. He's a waste of time and space.

Last Name

Yet her body tingled at the memory of the times they had spent together. All of those days, and nights in her quarters, nestled in his arms after a long shift. All of those wonderful stolen moments together during her breaks, and the hope the joy would never end, but they had finished and there was no turning back the sands of time.

All I want to do is be rid of him once and for all. He's not worth the pain he put me through, and I'm sure as hell not going to go through it again. Not for him. Not for anyone.

She had her career, and nothing else mattered.

The more she allowed her mind to linger on him, the faster her heart raced, and the higher her blood pressure spiked. Okay, she was guessing the last part, but it was a reasonable guess considering the stress he'd caused her. The gym. The faster she got herself into the gym and in a situation where she could beat a hapless bag until the seams split, the better it would be for all concerned.

A punching bag, a fight program, and she'd be ready to take on the entire sector again. Or at least the problems she faced on the station.

"Corina."

She froze at the sound of his voice, then continued down the corridor. Looking back would be a mistake. She'd only find herself facing him, potentially forced to talk to him, then they would argue. Maybe worse. She might throw a punch outside of the gym and Kraven would pin her hide to the nearest bulkhead. Besides, the gym was waiting for her, and she needed the workout. Maybe he'd get the hint and leave her alone?

Not bloody likely.

She wasn't going to turn and stare at him. He wasn't in charge, and she had a choice to ignore him or answer him. Her decision and she was strong enough to ignore him.

"Corina, I'm not going to vanish on you. You can either talk to me now I'll follow you all the way to the gym."

Damn him, he'd do it. He'd follow her regardless of what she wanted. Once she entered the gym, he'd lock the door behind them and get in her face.

Bastard. How the hell had he figured out where she was going? *Duh, because it's how you always handle stressful situations.* Kraven might have told him, which only added to the sting of betrayal. She stopped and turned to glare at him. "What did you want, Monroe? Was it to fuck me over again? Plan on getting me into bed and leaving before I wake up? Or were you going to leave a note this time? Have you learned to write?" Would it have killed him to leave a short note?

"Ah, we're back to that are we?"

Emotion flashed across his eyes. Doubt? Pain?

"I suppose I deserve it after the way we parted. I don't suppose it counts that I apologized? No, of course not. I know better than to ask." David Monroe stopped in front of her, his gaze traced her face, but it didn't move any lower. "You can at least let me ask a few civil questions, and those barbs are beneath you, or I thought they were. We did spend a few decent times together, after all. At least I believed we did. Shit, I'm not handling this well. Sorry. Okay. Let me try again here." He sighed and rubbed his temples before meeting her gaze again. "You're okay?"

"I'm fine for the most part as you can no doubt tell for yourself." She moved her weight over the balls of her feet and focused on her breathing. She wasn't going to lose her temper with him. She wasn't going to do this here. She was stronger than this and now was the time to show him what she was capable of. "Was there anything you wanted from me, David? Something important, or are you going to continue trying to find ways to prolong this excuse for a conversation?" She didn't look at him, not entirely, she wasn't going to make that mistake. Besides, she knew his appearance as well as she knew her own. "I have things I need to take care of, if I need to schedule you in, it would be best if you told me now."

Last Name

He had black hair, tied in the nape of his neck, but loose it fell below his shoulder blades. His eyes were the color of diamonds, sharp and hard, reflecting the light and colors from other sources except when he was aroused. Then they sparkled, glowed with an inner light which couldn't be ignored. She knew his body, the shape of his ass beneath her fingers, the play of his lips across her skin and she fought not to give into the tingles which threatened to play through her.

Her inner walls clenched in remembrance, heat played through her body, and she fought not to let it show. She wasn't going to allow this to happen to her, not this time. She couldn't let herself be weak, and he was a weakness, one which had plagued her for three years. One she would no longer allow a hold over her. No, she was stronger now, much stronger than she'd been when they'd first met.

Her nipples tingled, hardening into points beneath her shirt. The ache to be touched by him, held and caressed, grew with each passing moment. It threatened to destroy her from the inside, and she couldn't let him see her weaknesses. He'd use them. He'd see what was happening and before she had a chance to rebuild the walls, he'd worm his way into her heart and mind, leaving her helpless.

As he had before.

"Don't I warrant you turning to look at me when we talk?" His tone was cold and sharp. He took a deep breath, and his voice changed. Softer, a subtle plea behind the words. "Do you have so little control now you're going to keep your back to me? I assumed you were stronger. Look at me, please."

Her heart skipped a beat as she met his gaze for a moment. *Shit.* Too late, she'd already done it. Meeting his gaze for a moment was a mistake. One she paid for now. Heat surged again between her thighs, threatening to coat her inner walls with a hunger she wanted nothing to do with.

"We didn't part of the best of terms last time..." He began.

"That's one way of putting it. We had a wonderful night together, but then I woke up and you were gone." Anger flared at the memory, her hands clenching at her sides. No warning. No hints she'd been able to see either then or now. He'd simply vanished without a care for how she might react. "It wasn't exactly how I expected things to work out between us. But I guess you realized your mistake and fled before I awoke. Wonderful for you. Me – it took me a year before I found out who you really were, Monroe. You didn't tell me your real name. What the fuck did I do to deserve that? What did I do to hurt you?"

He blanched in front of her. "You could have at least given me a chance to finish. Shit, I was following orders…"

"Uh-huh, only following orders tell that to one who buys your lies or invent an original excuse. I don't buy that shit. I did once, never again. Especially not with a man who told me he was an Indie spacer. And now you're supposedly a fucking Indie Captain, the only orders they follow are the ones they set for themselves." She turned to leave, the memory of the shame, the way he'd left her, once more fresh in her mind. "Is your name Monroe, or is it another lie, another mask worn for you to get what you wanted from me? For once, I'd like to know the truth. Who the fuck are you? And who is it that gave you those orders you had to follow? Orders to leave me without a word."

"Damn you, it wasn't like that. I had a job, one I couldn't walk away from, and when my commanding officer called me, I had to leave. I wasn't given the time to let you know what was going on." He turned away from her, his head bowed slightly, hands resting on his hips.

Commanding officer? He was a freelance pilot – now captain- why would he have a commanding officer? Did he believe she'd accept his lines as an explanation? "Yes, of course, you had a commanding officer telling you what to do. All Indie pilots have one, right? And it was so important you couldn't tell your wife what was going on?" Those hands, those strong, knowing hands on her body, touching, stroking, parting her thighs until she moaned and shuddered in delight. No, she couldn't think of them being together again.

Too late.

David took a step back, his brow furrowed. He licked his lips nervously taking a deep breath before he spoke again. "I'm sorry."

"Is that all I'm worth? I'm your wife, Monroe. Check the records for yourself in case you're not entirely sure. We were married at Fartier Station the night before you went missing. Did none of what we together mattered to you?"

His brow furrowed, his voice uncertain as he met her gaze. "Yes, it did... does."

"Remember all the details now, do you?" She cleared the distance between them, her righthand snapping through the air, connecting with his left cheek before he had the chance to respond. "Remember how you wed me, fucked me, and left me, do you? How you crept out on our wedding night, leaving me naked in our bed after one final mercy fuck in the shower?"

His head snapped to the side, his eyes dazing for the moment before he growled and met her gaze. "Mercy fuck? Like hell it was."

"Oh, what would you call it then? You knew you were leaving, and you fucked me one last time before vanishing in the middle of the night." Gods above and below, she was letting him get to her.

"I had orders, I followed them. End of story." His hands clenched and relaxed rhythmically at his sides. "It was nothing personal. You know how this works when you're told what you're supposed to do."

"Nothing personal because you were only following orders, it's the defense of the weak and foolish." Her voice cold as ice, her jaw tight as she glared at him. She didn't shift her gaze away from him, her shoulders pressed back and chin lifted. "Of course, your orders will have included seducing, fucking, and marrying me. No doubt they were in the small print, right? You really must have loved your assignment. I bet they were all lining up, congratulating you on how lucky you were."

Mine. He was mine. I'd found the man I was going to spend the rest of my life with. I'd beaten the damned odds then he was gone. He didn't have the right to be angry with her. She was the one who had been hurt by all of this. He'd used her and she'd give anything to turn the time back to enjoy her final night with him again.

I'm a warrior, trained, and numbered amongst those of Mars. I should know better than this.

She did, that was part of the problem. Corina forced herself to take a deep, cleansing breath and struggled to push her emotions back under control. "I should thank you for showing me who you are, Monroe. Now you're on Freedom Station you can do us both a favor and sign the paperwork which will free us both from this obviously unwanted arrangement. I can have the papers to you in an hour, two at most. Divorce. It's the only viable option, wouldn't you agree? It doesn't matter if you do or don't, you're going to sign the papers as soon as I get them to you." Corina pushed her face into his, her gaze narrowed, eyes dark and tried to ignore the tempting caress of his breath across her lips. "Then you can get the hell out of my life once and for all. Is that clear?"

"Clear but is that all you want from me? Sign a few papers and vanish? I can't believe you'd be happy with such a simple arrangement."

She wasn't, but he didn't need to know. "Yes, it's all I want from you. The papers signed and this mess finally over and done with."

"It's not what I want, damnit. I want to make things right between us. I was wrong. What I did was wrong, and I refuse to accept this as the only possible solution."

"It's not about what you want, Monroe." Damn him for walking back into her life and expecting her to roll over and let him fuck her yet again.

Last Name

Silence settled between them for several long minutes before he took a deep breath and finally spoke again, his voice oddly calm. "Then I have a bargain to offer you, Corina. One which might get you what you want, if you're willing to take a chance?"

A bargain? What did he have up his sleeve this time? What right did he have to offer a deal in the first place? "And that would be?"

"We used to spar, remember?"

Oh hell yeah, she remembered. Corina forced herself to remain silent and simply nodded.

"I offer a fight, hand to hand. You win, I sign the papers, no argument. I'll be gone, and you'll be free to do whatever it is you want with the rest of your life."

"And if I lose the fight?" She inquired in a calm, crisp tone. Inside she shook. What if he won? What if she lost? *I'll be free of him — won't I?* "What then? What do you get out of this challenge?"

"Then you remain my wife. I'm not sure what it will mean for us, but we'll figure it out when or if we reach that point."

"You leave the station within two hours of losing the fight and signing the papers, agreed?" Her gaze narrowed, voice cold and clipped. "If it means you have to remain on your ship for the rest of your stay here, you don't set foot back on this station during this visit. No attempting to wriggle out of it or arrange a way around the agreement. I want this settled once and for all. I also want a warning the next time you're due to visit the station."

"Agreed."

No argument? Her heart sank, but she refused to let it taint her words. She wanted him gone, didn't she? *Yes. Hell yes. Now. Immediately… maybe.* "Agreed. The gym on the next level down, you know it?"

"Yes, I know it." He didn't turn away from her, but his hands had relaxed.

"I'll meet you in two hours. I have to change, or I'll be in more trouble with Kraven. Off duty means out of uniform and I'm not ready to push him again this soon, and you don't discuss this fight with him. Got it?" Kraven getting in the middle of things would only make matters worse.

If Kraven found out, Piotr would also be informed to tend any injuries resulting from the fight. If he knew, then others would become aware and before she had a chance to handle damage control half the station would know.

Okay, not half but enough to make life miserable for her over the coming months.

"Agreed."

Chapter Three

David stood watching as Corina lifted her head, turned smartly on her heel, and walked away without so much as glancing back at him. This wasn't how he'd planned on things working out between them. Okay, he hadn't exactly had a plan when she walked into Kraven's office, but the minute it had happened he'd known he couldn't walk away from her again.

He'd betrayed her by leaving, and all the excuses in the universe couldn't change it, but here and now he had a slim chance of winning her over again.

Well fuck.

Corina naked, bent over, her sweet backside presented to him or on her back, arms open as she welcomed his touch, his embrace. Hell, he'd take a quicky in a maintenance bay right now as long as it meant he'd be able to touch her again.

Leaving her, despite the orders, had been a mistake beyond measurement.

I can fix it.

He frowned, still staring down the corridor all though she was no longer in line of sight. Could this be fixed? Did he have a chance with Corina if he won the fight? Maybe. Winning would at least buy him time to talk to her. He wouldn't be bound by signing the paperwork.

Shit, the idea of signing those papers knotted his gut. He didn't want to lose her completely. Was this love? Real love? Or the need to keep her in his life?

Fuck if I know.

Gods, he needed a drink right now.

David Monroe shook his head and turned before he walked down the well-lit corridor. He had two hours before the fight but no idea what he would do with the time? He couldn't have a drink unless he wanted to give her an unfair advantage. Nor could he go and talk to Kraven because Corina was right, the man would get into the middle of the situation, and all hell would break loose. At best Kraven would give Corina another dressing down. At worst it would become station gossip, and she'd have to face it every time she tried to go about her daily duties.

No. He couldn't do that to her.

One simple fight and this would either all be over, or he'd find a way to win her over.

Uh huh. Right. Real simple.

Returning to the ship might be an option. He'd be able to check in and see if Blain had tried to contact him and he could change clothes. Fighting in street clothes didn't make sense when a gym was the location. He wasn't going to give her one damn iota of extra chances in this match, not with so much resting on the outcome.

My wife. Mine. I'm not going to give up on her. On this. On us.

He scowled at the idea. He'd had no problem walking away from her when the order had come down the line. He'd known it was on the cards when he'd gone through with the ceremony, yet he hadn't thought about delaying it.

He'd gone into it knowing he would hurt her.

Why? Why would anyone knowingly do that to a woman they cared for, and he'd known, he cared for Corina. It had taken him too long to realize caring didn't begin to describe things.

He loved her.

David fought against the need to punch the wall as he walked through the corridors and caught a 'chute down to the docking ring level. He'd questioned himself about it a time or two but had always pushed it to the back of his mind before he'd investigated it.

"Captain, welcome back. We weren't expecting you this soon." Amber met him moments after he entered the ship. "What's wrong?"

He smiled and tried to wipe his concerns from his features.

"No. I need to pick up a few things." Amber, she was always present when he entered the ship. Ready and waiting to serve him if needed – no not him, the ship, and any mission they had to complete.

"Nothing message wise save for a holding order."

He'd been expecting more, but he could wait. It wasn't as if he had anything else to do – except for the match against Corina. A fight he intended to win. "They'll contact us when they're ready to." He'd wait as long as he had to and if it gave him more time to figure things out with Corina then so much the better.

"Until then, Captain?"

"The usual."

Amber sighed and rubbed the back of her neck. "We appear as normal as possible and continue with daily activities. We watch for issues, report, and observe."

He flashed a grin and stopped outside of his quarters. "I'll be leaving the ship shortly. A few things to pick up, then I'll be gone. You'll be able to contact me if needed." He'd turn off his com during the fight, he didn't need the distraction it would offer if it went off at the wrong time.

"You have plans, Captain?"

"Meeting up with an old friend." He admitted though he wasn't about to tell Amber, or the rest of the crew, what was going on. Not until matters were settled one way or the other and then only if he had to. Shit, if he lost the fight, he wasn't about to admit it to them.

Will I be able to admit it to myself?

"Understood, Captain. I'll inform the crew." The woman snapped to attention, nodded once, then turned, disappearing down the corridor to leave David to his quarters.

By the time David sat down on one of the benches inside the gym, he was still trying to focus. He was early, but it didn't stop him from checking the time every few minutes. It was foolish to arrive with too much time to spare, but here he was, and leaving wasn't an option. If she walked in as he was leaving it would add a few more problems to the situation. She might take it as a sign he was giving up.

Yeah, would be just like her.

Perhaps he would be better off waiting outside of the gym? Would that appear more natural? Why did he care about what she believed?

I don't.

Like hell he didn't. He had nothing to prove. No, he'd wait. Corina would be here soon enough, then the real fight would begin.

He leaned back against the wall and closed his eyes. Mistake number one. Her face, her body, and the memory of the nights they'd shared, they all filled his mind as he sat. The way she'd moved for him, danced on his cock, playing with her breasts, and arching her back as she'd come for him. The sweet sound she'd made at the moment of pleasure, now echoed through his mind.

He growled, opening his eyes. Damn. He couldn't shut her out. He never would be able to shut her out not now he'd seen her again.

Do I want to?

No, he didn't. He had to win the fight if he wanted a chance of regaining his sanity.

"So much for sanity being an optional extra," he muttered and sat up.

The door slid open and closed the moment Corina entered the gym, focusing his attention entirely on his woman. He frowned slightly at the chime of the privacy lock but then nodded. It would be better with the door secured. If anyone walked in on the fight, they might misunderstand what was going on. An added bonus; they wouldn't have to leave the gym when the match was done.

Wouldn't do to have Kraven walk in at the wrong moment. I might have to kill him.

He blinked and tried not to stare, failing miserably. She'd taken the time to change her clothing, as she said she would do. Like him, she'd opted for gym wear, but hers enhanced her beauty and stripped her to the skin yet left her covered at the same time. At least where it counted. A sports bra cupped and lifted her ample breasts and a pair of skin-tight shorts molded to her firm backside.

She walked through the station wearing that?

How many men had seen her? Damn. Her outfit didn't leave much to the imagination, and if Kraven did walk in, he'd have to at least brain the guy for looking at his woman. Fuck, a man would have to be blind, deaf, and dumb not to be interested in Corina.

His cock thickened, pressing against his own sports shorts. It was going to make things interesting. He took a deep breath and tried to force his cock back under his command. Each step she took was a sensual challenge focused on him. She had to know what she was doing when she'd chosen the outfit, especially with who her mother was.

Be easy to strip her when we've finished. Maybe it's why she chose this outfit. She would select any weapon which would give her the advantage and if it meant using her body then so be it. She wasn't ashamed of doing such.

"Ah, I wasn't sure you'd be here." Corina's voice was gentle but professional. "At least not yet."

"Eager for the match, perhaps?"

"You're reading too much into it. We're both early, nothing more."

Interesting, he'd caught her off guard for the second time in one day. Not what he'd expected, but he could use it to his advantage. The more uncertain she was, the easier it would be to beat her in the fight unless she managed to put up the emotional walls her father would have taught her to build.

"Did you think I'd change my mind? Why wouldn't I be here waiting for you? I set the challenge after all, and I'm not the type to give up before I've begun." He forced himself to focus on her face. Any stripping would have to wait until after the fight. It would be best to push the images of her naked form to the back of his mind. Otherwise, he'd barely be able to focus.

"How could I forget?" She turned to stare at him, arching an eyebrow. "Remember the terms. I win, you sign the papers and leave. No arguments after the fact. I'm going to hold you to this no matter what excuses you try to come up with. Got it?"

"I haven't forgotten." How could he when so much was riding on this one confrontation. One fight and the matter would either be settled or begun anew. He could live with that either way. He'd have to.

"And the rules for the fight itself?" She kept her voice calm, her gaze steady. "I presume there will be an agreement on rules or at least the style of combat."

"Freestyle." David offered, watching her face for signs of a problem.

She paused a moment, her eyes clouding before she nodded. "Agreed."

Had there been a flicker of doubt? He couldn't be sure. Freestyle was always interesting. No rules save two. No death, no maiming.

Freestyle.

She hadn't expected that. It would make the fight interesting, and it was just as well she'd locked the door. The only way anyone else could walk in now was with a security override. As for the fight, she'd win. She had a lot of practice under her belt, more than most women outside of the Peacekeepers or those of Mars or Valhalla. She simply had to remember what she'd learned and not let her emotions get the better of her. She had a lot riding on this fight, and she wasn't about to give up on her chance of true freedom.

Corina moved into the center of the gym and rolled out her shoulders as she walked. She'd already worked out the stiffness, and her muscles were loose, ready for whatever he might throw at her. She'd spent the time in her room in the form of walking meditation her mother, not her father, had taught her as a child. Odd how she'd never thought she'd find a way to merge the two sets of traditions.

Now she waited for him in the center of the gym, her weight on the balls of her feet, her knees flexed, her gaze fixed on his every move. "Ready?"

"Yes," he moved to stand a few feet away from her. "And when I win, you and I will have a long talk about our marital status, so there's no confusion here. I've no intention of signing the papers. You're my wife, and I intend to do whatever is in my power to help you remember the man you fell in love with. The man who still loves you despite the fact I've been a complete and utter ass."

His words were a weapon, but they were ones not easily ignored. Fuck, did he know how hard it had been for her when he'd walked out? How many doubts he'd left her with? How she'd had to run to her father's people before she'd finally been able to come to terms with what had happened? She'd thrown herself into training, into the ways of her people only to realize she couldn't go back through the training without surrendering an entire year of her life. With too many regrets she'd left before entering the refresher program.

If he had been ordered away and it wasn't an excuse he expected her to believe, then why couldn't he tell her who had given him the order? Why hide behind the excuse when he had always been adamant he was nothing more than an Indie pilot turned captain? He couldn't have it both ways.

Gods, how she'd wished her father had been present, the way he had been when she'd been a child, but at least his clan had welcomed her back with open arms. They'd given her enough to refocus her heart and soul, or so she believed until David had walked back into her life.

Father. Damn you for leaving me when I needed you the most.

Damn your pride for fighting when you weren't ready to go back into the field. When you would have ordered others to rest until they had been cleared by the med techs. Damn you for dying.

No, she didn't have time for this. She had to focus on David and the fight. Nothing else mattered now. She closed her eyes for a moment, a breath, and opened them, her emotions back under control. She wasn't going to rise to the bait. Not this time.

Not this time.

He moved without another word. His weight shifted onto his left foot as he struck out with his right hand, palm open.

She blocked the blow quickly enough, with one arm, striking out toward his ribs with her free hand, only to find her wrist caught. Weight shifted as they moved together, and for a moment she believed she'd found a way free of his grasp. The old forms coming back to her as if she'd never left the practice mats.

David shifted his stance and pulled. Before she realized what was happening, Corina felt herself half flying through the air and over his hip. Instinct took over, and she was rolling, then up and back to her feet before she realized what she'd done. She turned on the balls of her feet, facing him as he charged toward her.

His shoulder connected with her stomach, forcing her back. Her hands clenched, meeting together in a double fist she brought down, hard, against his neck. She'd barely had the time to strike as her backside hit the floor. She twisted beneath him, slamming her knee into his stomach only to be rewarded by a grunt of pain from the man above her.

She growled, twisting, striking a second time, her knee hitting his ribs before she scrambled out from beneath his grasp. A hand grabbed her ankle. Iron hard, unyielding though she kicked and struggled to try and break free.

David.

Shit, when did I start thinking of him as David and not Monroe? He's the enemy. I have to win this fight. I'm not going to spend the rest of my life tied to him. It's not happening.

Last Name

A second hand tightened around her ankle. She kicked harder, aiming for his head, two blows connecting with loud grunts of pain but the third missed.

Fuck. This wasn't in the plan.

The grip on her ankle twisted. Shards of pain shot through her limb as she tried to lash out at him again. This wasn't happening to her. It wasn't happening. She knew how to fight. How the hell had she lost this fight?

She hadn't, not yet. Not as long as she was willing to punch, kick, and claw her way free of his grasp. It wasn't over.

The mind is willing, the flesh and spirit have other ideas?

No, this wasn't happening. She couldn't back down or give up like this. He had no right to win, not after everything he'd done to her.

But I want him to win.

He moved over her, pinning her to the floor, his hands settling on either side of her head, chasing away the argument which distracted her from the fight. His body, an unyielding weight above her, brushed against her breasts and thighs, sending tingles through her firm flesh. Panic flared. She twisted, trying to find a means to be free of him, but it only made matters worse.

Heat surged between her thighs, throbbing into her clit with a desire so real she bit into her bottom lip. She didn't need the distraction her body was providing. Push past this, she had to push past this before she lost her focus completely.

"You fought better than this once, Corina. What happened to you?" He smiled down at her, his gaze gentle. "Perhaps you didn't want to win? You want to find yourself under me again, with my cock buried deep inside you."

Her answer stilled in her throat. She couldn't tell him what she didn't know. Instead, she fought, struggling beneath him. Her knees slamming into his ribs, but she couldn't gain enough momentum to strike effectively. All he did was grunt and continue to hold her beneath him.

He'd won. Despite her experience, he'd beaten her.
Like hell he has.

She forced herself to relax a touch and smiled up at him. She could do this, and once she had him distracted, she'd be able to change the rules of the game. "Enjoying?" She rolled her hips beneath him. Could he feel the heat? Yes, he had to, it was obvious, and now she could feel the liquid desire coating her nether lips and soaking into her panties. He'd be able to smell her arousal by now, and maybe it would distract him long enough that she'd be able to break free.

His cock thickened, pressing down against her body. "I always did enjoy holding you, love. You're a beautiful, sensual woman in the arms of the right man and I know I'm that man."

"Only holding me?" She licked her lips slowly, then parted them, arching her neck. Hope rose as she felt grip loosening. "Or did you enjoy a more sensual moment? An intimate time shared between us."

"More, a lot more. What we shared. All of your groaning, the naked flesh, the way it all worked between us." He growled the words and leaned closer, his lips only a breath away from hers. "I haven't forgotten how you would move for me or the sounds you made when we made love."

"When we fucked." She watched his eyes widen at her words. Good, she'd hit him where it hurt yet her stomach knotted, and a part of her shrank away at the hurt as it flashed across his eyes. "Call it what is was, lover. We fucked everywhere we possibly could in my quarters, and a few places besides."

"We made love." He protested, though his words lacked certainty. "I was your husband, and we made love."

"No, it requires you being in love with me, David. You felt something deep and meaningful toward me, which is a joke. We both know it wasn't a part of your plans. As for me, yes, I loved you, but I accept now it was one-sided." She rolled her hips again and pressed up against his body. She had to stay with this idea if she wanted to distract him long enough to throw him off. "We. Fucked. Nothing more. Get over it already."

He growled in delight, his eyes half closing for a moment, then opened again, wariness flickering in his gaze. "I don't know that I can."

Corina wriggled beneath him, her gaze locking with his. She knew what she had to do, but it was a chance she'd only get once in this fight. "And what took you so long to find me again, David? It would have been easy enough to hunt me down because of my career path." She added a soft purr to her words. "If you remembered what we did if it was special to you, why didn't you come and find me? I might have forgiven you if you'd arrived earlier. I might have welcomed you back." A lie? Perhaps, perhaps not. She could think about it later. Right now, she had to focus on dealing with David.

"I didn't know where to look. I presumed you would have found a way to prevent me from searching for you." A small frown formed across his brow. "No, it's not true. I assumed you'd returned to Gaea, and didn't think I would be welcomed. If you'd been on Mars, the chances of seeing you were non-existent. Not after what had happened between us. I know how violent things can get with the clans if one of their own has been hurt. Shit, for all I knew your family would hunt me down and deal with my transgression."

No, she'd be the one to do it if he'd followed her before her temper had been brought back under control. She'd dreamed of carving his heart out more times than she cared to admit to right now, but that was in the past. Wasn't it?

"We'll never know what would have happened now, will we?" She kept her gaze fixed with his, parting her lips before she swiped the tip of her tongue over her lips.

"No, I suppose not." His gaze narrowed as he watched the path of her tongue.

She slipped her arms free, moving as if to wrap them about his neck in an embrace, but struck instead. She slammed the heel of both hands against his chin, seeking to drive his head back and up. As he cried out, she twisted beneath him, trying to roll him away from her, and at that moment she succeeded.

The weight shifted, and she rolled free, scrambling to her feet, her gaze fixed on David as her heart sank. *I shouldn't have done that.*

He groaned, rolling in the opposite direction before he pushed up to his knees, shaking his head to clear it. "Bitch."

"What was your first clue?" She smiled and kept her weight on the balls of her feet, ready for his next move. Whatever he had planned, she'd be prepared for him this time.

She had to be ready for him if she wanted to hold onto her already tenuous control.

David shook his head, trying to clear it as he stepped back and tried to focus once more. Fuck, he should have seen it coming as if she'd actually welcome his arms around her once more. No, that ship had long since sailed despite her heated words, but he'd fallen for it because it was what he wanted to believe could happen. He'd fucking fallen for it, and she'd done well, pulling him in close with dark, delicious words turned his cock rock hard. This was the woman he had denied for three years, and yet now he wanted her more than he'd desired anyone or anything in his life.

His wife. His lover. The missing part of his soul and yet she wanted to be free of him, and it was his fault. If he'd questioned his orders and listened to his heart this once, then maybe he could have found a way to be with her instead of carving out her heart and walking out on what should have been the happiest night of their lives.

Instead, he'd obeyed orders, used it as a crutch and not walked away. He'd run.

Afraid.

Last Name

Yeah, okay, he could see it now. He'd been afraid of the commitment he'd stumbled into. Afraid of spending the rest of his life with one woman though he knew Corina was the right woman for him. He shook his head again, clearing the stars from his vision before he turned his full attention to the woman.

Coward.

Gods. He'd been a complete coward. He hadn't had the guts to tell her no about the marriage. Or to wait until she'd woken up before he'd left. A thousand things he'd done wrong in all of this but running away had been the biggest. He knew it, and it was time to make things right.

Corina stayed out of immediate grabbing range, her presence taunted him, and he wasn't going to let her get away from him. Not this time.

Mine.

Fuck, he could still feel the damned blow. Fine, she wanted to play it this way, he'd gladly oblige her. Then he'd teach her a lesson in how the game was supposed to be played. He had more than a few tricks up his sleeve he'd never shown her, and now it was time to take the gloves off. He grinned at the idea, watching Corina as she moved, slowly, around the gym, her steps light and practiced. This wasn't going to be as easy as he'd first thought it would be.

He reached for her, but she moved away again, keeping out of his reach and forcing him to stalk after her, to try and corner her.

"Still dancing away from me, Corina? Not willing to come in close for a real fight? I never took you for a coward." It was an insult which would typically work, pulling her in and tempting her to rash moves. Or it would have done three years ago. She'd changed; they both had. "You never used to be this cautious. You rose to the challenge and met me head on. What's changed? Do I frighten you that much?"

She smiled but said nothing.

Okay, she'd always been smart, and now she'd learned not to react to his barbs. It didn't work, he'd have to rethink his plans.

She'd always been intelligent, and now she proved it beyond a doubt. Why waste breath on an argument, when there was a fight to be had? Her gaze followed each shift of his weight. She hadn't forgotten any of it. The way she moved brought back too many memories. She was both Gaean and a child of Mars, combined in one body, strength and sensuality in the shape of a woman he had held, tasted, kissed, and taken.

Fine, he'd have to push things. He watched the pattern of her moves, waiting for the opening. He knew how to do this. He'd done it in other fights, and he couldn't hold back this time, not if he wanted to keep Corina in his life.

I need her.

He shadowed her moves, watching but unable to touch. Each time he grabbed for her and missed, his frustration grew until he growled, the sound low in the back of his throat. No. He couldn't let his frustration get the better of him.

Shit. She'd learned how to push his buttons, and this was one of them.

Smart, smart woman.

How to pull her in? She knew his moves or the old ones at least.

Don't try it. Watch. Listen. Learn.

A pattern to her moves? Maybe. A small repeat of movements her body had fallen into. A flaw another might have missed if they hadn't sparred with her before, but he had.

There it was again. A slight dip, the shift of weight to her right foot before she stepped to the right and immediately took two paces to the left. The third time he'd seen it, and it was the opening he needed. All he had to do was wait for the next set of steps.

"Getting tired, Monroe?" Her voice was calm but slightly breathy. Same as she was during sex.

Focus on the fight. Not sex. Not hot, sweaty, naked, grunting sex.

She moved left, her step not as strong as it should have been, and he turned, shifting his weight onto his right foot, lashing out with his left until he caught the back of her leg. She cried out, crumpling to the floor, one hand clutching her aching knee.

"Bastard." She cried out, rubbing her knee, her gaze blazing in fury. "You fucking bastard."

"Yes I am, and in every sense of the word, I've never lied to you about." He smiled. It had worked. "And this time your enjoyable wriggling games aren't going to pull you free."

"Like hell. I'm not giving up. You don't get to win. You don't get to hurt me again." Corina rolled, trying to come up to her feet but he was ready for her this time. He lashed out, grabbing the back of her neck with one hand and used it to force her to her feet, but under his terms. She wriggled, jamming elbows back at him. It didn't work though he grunted with the blows. With his free hand, he wrapped an arm about her body, trapping her arms to her body as he held her against him.

Against him with her firm, round ass pressed against his hard and oh so eager cock. The heat from her body seeped into his, taunting him, promising him far more than he'd been willing to think about except in brief, weak moments.

"Yield." He whispered against her ear. "I'm not going to hurt you this time."

"Not fucking lightly." She snarled, struggling in his grasp. "I don't believe you. I won't believe you."

"You can't break free, love." He nibbled softly down the length of her neck. He'd hurt her, he understood it, and he'd do all he could to prove to her it wasn't going to happen again. "You're safe with me now."

She stiffened against him. "You can't do this to me…"

"But I can. I won, you're my wife, and I believe we have a lot of catching up to do."

Chapter Four

He'd won. How the hell had that happened? She'd watched for his moves, checked for openings, covered herself carefully, and he'd still found a weak moment. One which shouldn't have been present, one he'd taken advantage of and now she paid for it unless she could find a way to wriggle free of his grasp. She'd covered every damn opening she could think of and a few more besides.

This shouldn't have happened.

Had she let it happen?

Had it been a deliberate act by her?

Gods above and below, had she wanted him to win?

No, of course not. I'd never let him win no matter what he might think. I'm not the woman he left behind. I'm stronger now, and I don't want him in my life again. No, she wouldn't have let him win so what had happened? She frowned, trying to make sense of the situation as a shiver of desire worked its way through her body.

All she could think of was the man pinning her down, the slight give of the gym floor beneath her and the artificial lighting cast shadows across his face. She took a deep breath, tasting the slight metallic edge to the filtered air – a scent you became used to after spending time on a ship or station – and shivered. Her entire body was alive. For the first time in three years, she was truly alive, and she didn't know how to handle it.

Why was this happening to her?

Did it matter? She'd lost and had to find a way to break free of him. Except she couldn't. She'd agreed to this, and she wasn't the type to break her word no matter how badly she wanted to right now.

Her body tingled at the way he held her. No, more than tingled, her body remembered his touch and wanted more, and she'd already been aroused the last time he had pinned her to the floor. Excited and ready to part her thighs for him until her common sense had taken over. Still, she remembered the time they had shared together before he'd walked out on her. All of the pleasure and delights they had known together.

A part of her wanted to experience it again. The part which needed to be as far away from him as possible before it surrendered willingly to whatever he wanted. Escape wasn't going to happen if she stayed in his arms. The longer he held her, the more she wanted his touch, all of his caresses no matter the danger they offered her.

"Well?"

"Fine, I yield." She growled out the words. *No. No, I don't. I don't want to yield.* She had to take control, fight back, conquer him, then have what she wanted. She could do. It would answer the need itching its way under her skin and down, between her thighs.

His grip didn't ease. "I was beginning to wonder if I'd have to spank you before you saw sense. It wouldn't have been the first time you needed such a push."

Her breath hitched at his word. He'd spanked her before, during their time together and she'd loved it but now she hated the idea, didn't she? He had no right to suggest such a thing. Not when he knew how she reacted to him walking back into her life. "Y-you know better than that. Spanking me would only piss me off." Not a wise idea, not with the images she now dealt with. David. On his back. Her straddling him, cutting off clothing before she rode him, claimed him once more. If there was to be one in charge in their relationship this time, it would be her.

Won't be a damned relationship. He's already proved he can't maintain one without running away. He'll try to get laid then he'll leave, in the middle of the night, when I'm asleep like he did last time. She couldn't stand the idea of history repeating itself. She wasn't strong enough to handle the loss again.

"I recall a time when spanking you had another effect on you." He growled against her neck. "When you welcomed correction from time to time. It was how you knew who was in charge, like the night we parted. I remember the water sliding over your ass, an ass warmed by my hand."

"Things change," she tensed in his grasp. *It hadn't happened that way. If it did, I won't let it happen again.* "You won, let me go. I've got better things to do with my time. I might be off duty for a time, but it doesn't mean I don't have shit to see to." Such as the piles of messages in her inbox.

"Let you go? No, I don't think it's going to happen." He loosened his grip a touch. "But I think we need to discuss this somewhere with a little more privacy, don't you?"

"Privacy for what?" Her heart skipped a beat. Dumb question, she knew what he wanted. For a moment she was tempted to remind him the room was locked, but it wouldn't stop the station from recording what went on in here...

The record of David beating her would be bad enough, a recording of them engaged in sex was one reminder she could live without. Especially as she lacked the security clearance to wipe it from the station's memory, which meant if an officer with higher clearance did a random check.

That's the last thing I need right now.

"I think you already know the answer to that one, love." He finally released his grip on her and stepped away. "Do we retire to your quarters, or do we continue this here where anyone can walk in?" The look in his eyes made it clear he didn't care which option she picked.

Talk, yeah, okay he wanted to do more than talk, and they both knew it. They were married, but they weren't on good terms, he couldn't expect more than a conversation from her. Yet he *would* expect such. He'd want to touch her. He'd want to push her into a sexual situation. She wasn't ready for it, not with him, not with anyone. She hadn't let anyone near her, sexually, since David had walked out on her.

Yet her inner walls clenched as he touched her arm, resting his fingers lightly on her sweat coated skin. She edged away from him a step, but it wasn't enough, he followed her, once again touching her arm. "Please, don't…"

"I think you mean, please more." Monroe let go of her. "But you still haven't answered my question. Where should we head to?"

"Fine, there's a café a short walk from here." Her breasts ached for his touch, a liquid heat rolling between her thighs. She squirmed slightly, trying to shut it out but her body had a mind of its own. "I could do with a drink anyway." At least in public, they'd both be forced to behave and keep a safe distance from her. Besides, she needed a drink before she called it a night.

Distance, a safe distance where you can't grab me that easily.

Yes, alright, it's what she needed, but a public setting was the next best thing.

"No, we need privacy." He moved in front of her, folding his arms across his chest. A living wall who blocked her exit and forced her to breath in the scent of sweat clinging to his body. "Unless you want your friends to hear the glorious details of the relationship we shared? All those sweet, intimate moments with you spread beneath me or sitting on me. The way you presented your naked body for my pleasure or the way you whimpered when I took hold of your hair? Is that what you want them to hear?"

Yes, she remembered all too well what it was like.

Shit. Her heart plummeted into the pit of her stomach. He'd do it too. Damned man would make sure the entire station could hear each intimate detail of the life they had shared. He'd delight in watching her squirm and color in shame.

Would it be too bad to experience it again? To know what it was like to spend time with him, naked, on her bed, the floor, against the wall, anything where she could let down the walls and be his for one last time?

To hell with the agreement, she'd still fight the marriage. Being with him for the rest of her life wasn't on the cards. Not now. Not ever. This was where she was drawing a line in the sand and he could live with it.

And so can I. Once he's off the station I can close the doors once and for all.

Not if she didn't handle this the correct way. If she managed to persuade him to leave the station, he might come back, and she wasn't about to run. No. This was her home – at least for as long as she was assigned here – and she wasn't going to go into hiding.

"Fine, we'll go to my quarters then, but you will respect they are my quarters and not your personal playground." She turned, heading for the door of the gym. Maybe she could lock him out of her room? No, it wouldn't work either. She'd made an agreement and had to go through with it. "But this is to talk and nothing else in case you missed the message in my earlier words. I'm not letting you into my bed, got it? That's off limits."

Who needs a bed? We certainly didn't.

His gaze narrowed slightly. "It depends on what we both want, doesn't it?"

Corina shivered at his words and glanced away from him. No games. No leeway. Conversation, reality check, and with luck, he'd back off and let her get on with her life.

It was a slim shot, but it was the only one she had right now.

Talk? Was she serious with the way her nipples had pebbled blatantly beneath her clothing and the aroma of arousal clinging to her skin? Did Corina not understand the signals her body was giving off? No, there'd be a lot more than talking going on before they'd finished. He could smell her arousal, the sweet scent built between her thighs and couldn't be ignored. She was as desperate for more as he was. Fine, he could live with that, all he had to do was persuade her sex was the next logical step between them.

Last Name

Their marriage wasn't over, and Corina needed to realize the truth.

Spanking her would be a start. She might remember who was the leader in our relationship and how much she enjoyed it. The women of both Mars and Gaea both respected a strong man in their beds as long as the man in question didn't disrespect them. They knew, in a relationship, there could only be one leader, and in their case, it had been him. Once she'd been able to let the walls down, he'd seen a side to her few had ever known existed.

One he had known before.

A side where she was a sweet, willing, delightfully sensual woman ready to surrender to the heat which built between them whenever they were together. His balls tightened. She was a woman who had deep appetites, and he could remember most of them. Such as the way she'd lifted her body to him, her thighs parted, ankles back over her own head, back tight as she'd pressed against him. She was strong, beautiful, and knew how to stand up to him when it mattered.

The last thing Corina had ever been was weak; she'd been submissive in the bedroom, when the mood struck them both, but never weak.

Cold sweat beaded across his flesh, and he forced the image away, burying it for now at least. Time enough for this later, after they'd talked.

Corina led the way out of the gym, he had no idea where her quarters would be. His ship wasn't an option either, too many people around who'd ask awkward questions and until matters had been sorted between them, he'd have to be careful. Okay, he was now in a position where he was the ranking officer on his ship, but it didn't mean he wanted to answer questions before he was ready to deal with the fallout.

When things were stable between them, then it would be different. He'd stand in front of his crew and introduce her as his wife. He wasn't sure how they'd take the information, but he'd deal with it when it happened.

No more hiding.

No, he wasn't going to hide or lie about who he was. At least not with Corina. If it got him in trouble with Blain and the rest of the higher-ups then so be it. His crew would accept it, and Blain had made it clear he didn't want to lose Monroe from the service.

And therein lay another problem. Corina was assigned to *Freedom Station* as a member of their peacekeeping force, and she wasn't likely to give up on her career without a damn good reason. The need for experienced peacekeepers on the station was one he was all too aware of. Between bar fights, troubles with the twin worlds, traders, raiders, smugglers and more, the station couldn't afford to lose a single peacekeeper. Which left a problem he had to figure it out. There had to be a way as he didn't plan on leaving her behind again. Not this time.

Was there anything else he should know about her? About her life? Was there a man? They'd been apart for some time, she could be attached for all he knew. She could, by now, have another man in her life and in her bed. He frowned, the thought an unpleasant one.

No, it went way beyond unpleasant. They were married, he'd run the check during the two-hour break, and as such, she was his. If she had a lover warming her bed then he'd – he'd what?

Sulk?

Pout?

Stomp his feet?

Beat the bastard into a bloody pulp. Then I'll find a use for his entrails. Maybe a new form of decoration? It might catch on. An entire new line in men's fashion. Sure, right... It was an idea but not one which would gain him any new friends on the station.

"Is there anyone in your life I should know about, as your husband I mean?" He'd forced the unwanted words into life. "An intimate friend, I mean." The words threatened to stick in his throat.

Last Name

Her shoulders stiffened at his words. "And you'd need to know why?"

"If my wife is —"

"The wife you walked out on has been free to do whatever, or whoever, the fuck she wanted. I suggest you learn to live with it unless you want to change your mind and sign the papers." She turned to meet his gaze, her voice a low whisper. Her eyes turned cold, flinty as she glared at him. "You wanted this conversation in private?" Her jaw was tight, the color draining from her normally olive tinted skin. "Or have you changed your mind. If you have then we can go and discuss this at the café I mentioned earlier."

"Fair point." He struggled to keep the growl from his voice. He glanced down the corridor. Only a few shadows at the far end but no one close enough to overhear what was being said. At least as long as they didn't start a shouting match.

Not her style. Or mine.

He sighed and rubbed the back of his neck. She had a lover, obviously. What did he expect? More to the point, what was he going to do about it once he found out who it was?

Kill him. Slowly.

Where the hell had that idea come from? He didn't go around killing people, not without cause. Maybe if someone started a fight with him, he'd be forced to take it to the extreme. Or if his ship was attacked. Sure, he'd defend his friends...

Alright, maybe he did go around killing people on occasions. *Like now.*

The guy, whoever he was, who was involved with Corina, likely didn't know she was married. He hadn't known until today. He couldn't precisely kill a man for it. He could, however, have words with Corina for not filling them in on the small details.

I'm still going to kill the bastard as soon as I find out who he is.

Except, she wouldn't have hidden her previous relationship from whomever she was involved with, it wasn't in her nature. She might have told them the full truth; she was married, and her husband had left her the morning after the commitment had been made. Yeah, alright, that was more like it. The guy would know exactly what he had been getting himself into. And – and he still couldn't kill the guy for it.

He could, but it wasn't justified.

Ug, I man, you woman, you touch my woman, you die, ug. Me bring home meat, woman cook, ug. We then fuck like bunnies.

Okay, more detail he hadn't wanted to know about himself.

"In here."

Corina's voice brought him back into focus. They'd moved H away from the commercial area of the station, or at least one part of it. He glanced down the corridor at the doors, all of them identical, he assumed he led into various quarters.

His wife had already keyed in her code, and the door had slid open, but he waited for her to enter it first. It was, after all, her home. She frowned, staring at him for a moment before seeming to realize what he was doing.

"Fine," she muttered. "Coming in or staying out?"

He flashed a grin and walked into the chamber. Only when the door closed behind him did he get the chance to take a look around the main room of her small quarters. And damn, did he mean small. This didn't feel right. She was a peacekeeper and should have been entitled to larger quarters, what was going on?

She'd had more room than this as a very junior officer on a much smaller station. He didn't understand why she had been quartered in a place like this.

"You appear confused," Corina settled down at her workstation and watched him.

"You're a Lieutenant, right?" He took a slow look around the room again before turning his attention fully to the waiting woman. "That's the rank I heard you addressed by, and the insignia on your uniform."

"Yes," she nodded slightly. "I am."

"Why are you living in such a small space?" He glanced

pointedly around. "You're entitled to a bigger set of quarters, aren't you? I mean this feels off." He'd seen Ensigns with bigger quarters and *Freedom Station* wasn't exactly small. The station was large with talk about it being expanded. Between it being the neutral point between the two warring worlds, and the last station or outpost before you ventured into Independent territory, the station dealt with enough traffic to warrant an expansion.

What the hell was he missing here?

"Never saw the need for more space. There's only me, after all, and what would I do with more room? I don't carry around a lot of clutter. Don't you remember?" She answered calmly, barely glancing at him. "No, I guess you were more focused on other things."

He tried to picture her old place. A memory of the few bits and pieces she'd kept on display, but those were gone. No holos, no trinkets from her other duty stations, no reminders from her home world though he was certain he'd seen such things the last time they'd been together.

Something was missing. A piece he knew should be on one of her walls, or on her desk.

His gaze narrowed, a scowl replacing the frown. "Where's the dagger I gave you?"

"Ah, you remember then?" She folded her arms and leaned back in her chair. "I'm surprised you remember anything about our time together beyond getting laid. Still, it's nice to know you can think on occasions."

He bit back the growl as it tried to force its way free. No. He wasn't going to lose his temper. It's what she wanted as it would give her the upper hand. Not happening.

His gaze moved to her breasts, then back to her face. Damnit, he knew better than to let the move distract him. "Yes, of course I remember the dagger. I bought it for you. Where is it?" The look on her face when he'd given her the ancient dagger from Mars was scene he'd never forget. He'd haggled for hours after making sure it was an original blade and not a replica. He'd polished it, found a box, and wrapped it for her before presenting the gift.

He'd never forget her smile, nor would he forget the kiss and all that followed.

"I got rid of it, as I did with all the other junk you picked up for me. I didn't see a reason to keep it." Her jaw tightened, eyes narrowed as she glared at him. "After all, the man who bought it for me didn't think me worth waking to say goodbye. Why would anything you gave me be worth keeping?"

The words lanced through him sharper than any blade. "I see."

"Now, let's get this over and done with. I'm not going to stay married to you. It's not going to work. You walked out, and frankly, I don't trust you as far as I can throw you. I'm expecting you to pull the same damn shit again as soon as you get 'orders' to head out." Her words were clipped and cold, but her eyes, a flicker in her eyes which denied the coldness of her words.

"Do you still love me?" *Dumb bloody question.* How could she after the way he'd treated her but he had to ask. She hadn't listed it as a reason why things wouldn't work between them. Still, he had to know the truth. He had to know what was going on with her before he made a final choice.

Love me. Please, say you still love me.

"What the fuck has it got to do with anything?" She snapped, her lips pressed into a tight, thin line. "We're here to discuss the divorce papers, not emotions which might cloud the issue. Sign and be done with it already." She gestured at the papers before she folded her arms beneath her breasts.

No denial. Interesting.

"Ah, you do still feel a bond between us." He took a step toward her. She'd have denied it if she felt nothing, or rolled her eyes. Acted in a manner which would make it clear it was over once and for all.

"I never said that." She bristled, turning away from him. "Don't put words in my mouth, David."

Last Name

"Say it now. I don't want any misunderstandings between us, Corina. We need to get everything out in the open then we can get on with this and make the right decisions." *You can't say it because it wouldn't be true.* She wouldn't be reluctant to bring the words to life unless she still believed the bond existed between them.

"Why won't you sign the papers, David?" She met his gaze. "You know we don't belong together. We haven't for a long time. It's why you didn't come back for me and made no attempt to contact me." She pushed out of the chair and stepped away from him. "Sign them and get out of my life. My life is here, with the peacekeepers. Yours is gods alone know where. It's not like you ever told me the truth about what you were doing, did you?"

She was right.

David reached out, grabbing her upper arm. "No, no more dancing away from me, Corina. I had orders. Sure, they sucked, but what was I supposed to do, disobey them? Stay on the station and wait for them to issue the damn arrest warrant?"

"Yes. No. I don't know. Arrest warrant for what? Shit, you haven't told me, have you? At least you could have taken the damn time to explain to me what was going on." She tried to yank free of his grip. "Get your fuckin' hands off me. I didn't let you in here to push me around. I don't know who you work for. And don't give me a line about being an Indie captain. I don't buy it, not anymore. I'm not the gullible woman you wedded and bedded."

"Get my hands off you? No, I don't think so." He grabbed her other arm and pulled her in. She deserved answers, as did he. "As you won't answer my question, I'll have to find out another way to get the answers I need from you."

Her eyes widened, pulse spiking – or at least his grip said it spiked. He had the desired effect on her.

"Let me go. You can't do this to me in my own room. This – this is wrong." She struggled, trying to break free of his grasp, but it wasn't happening. "Get the hell off me. Now."

"No."

"This is assault." She forced the words out from between clenched teeth. "Back the fuck off."

"Report me and have me arrested. You have every right to contact your people and hand me over for this. Have me arrested, Corina." He pulled her against his chest. "But we both know you won't do that. You wouldn't bring this up to anyone else no matter how much you want to bluster at me."

"Because anyone who's assaulted in the privacy of their own quarters has to have overwhelming evidence it wasn't consensual." She tugged again and growled her hands clenched into tight fists.

He couldn't deny it, there had been too many instances of he said/she said, but it was still an option for her. "Perhaps, in this case, it's also because a part of you does want this because you know I'd stop if your protests were real. I don't rape, Corina you know me. I might push, press, but I don't rape. Tell me you really want me to stop. Look in my eyes and tell me it's truly over between us." He leaned down, brushing his lips against hers. "You can't. I know you can't because you want to remember, to enjoy what we once had, Corina."

"No." Corina pressed her lips together in a tight, thin line, her eyes flashing, changing rapidly he had no clue what she was thinking or feeling. He wanted to shake her, to get her to talk to him, tell him what was going through her mind, but it wouldn't help. Instead, he released his grip on her left arm, and slid his hand into her hair, fisting it. She arched, her eyes snapping open as he knew small shards of pain played through her scalp, bringing tears to her eyes.

"Yes," he whispered against her lips, breaking the kiss only a fraction. Gods, he wanted her. "Now, tell me you want me to stop, and I will. That's all you have to do, Corina. Tell me. I don't push where I'm not wanted, and I can tell the difference between what you say you want and what you actually want."

Corina opened her mouth but said nothing and closed it once more.

"You can't, can you?" He released her other arm, though one hand remained in her hair. "You can't tell me to stop. No more than you can activate your security system because you know what will happen, all the questions you'd face." He wasn't being fair. "There's proof you agreed to this talk, and you could easily get me out of here by telling me you don't want me here. Say it. Tell me you want me to stop, you want me to leave, you have no doubt me leaving is what you desire."

"No. I can't." Her voice quiet.

"Why?" He slid his hand out from her hair and cupped her cheek. "Tell me why you can't do it."

She swallowed hard, her gaze flickering from his eyes to his lips and back again. "There's a connection between us." Corina shook her head softly. "I don't like it, but I'm not going to lie about it either. Maybe it's the memories of the time we shared, I don't know. Maybe I'll never know, but it's undeniable."

"It's all I needed to know." He covered her lips with his own once more.

Corina appeared to tense for a moment, then relaxed and slipped her arms about his neck. The three years since they'd married and he'd vanished, fell away as if they'd never been. She was here in his arms, they were together once more, and it was all going to be alright. For a moment, she stopped, trying to pull back from his kiss until he tightened his grip on her afresh. But he broke the kiss again, frowning.

"What's wrong?"

"You walked out on me, and what's to stop you from doing it again? A quick roll in the sack and you'll be gone, right? Is that your plan? Have you another mission which will pull you away? A new set of orders and I'll wake up again to an empty bed?"

"It's not like that, Corina." Gods, he hadn't wanted to start this fight again, not when he'd gained ground however small a gain it might be. Did she believe he'd walk out on her without warning again?

"Then tell me what it is like. I want to go into this with my eyes wide open this time. Not caught in the dark at the wrong moment. I don't want to roll over, expecting to find you, to find out you've not only left my quarters but the station without a word. Is it too much to ask?" Corina demanded as she blinked and fought against the tears which glistened in her eyes.

"I'm not going to leave without warning again. Even if I only have a few hours' notice, I'll still come and find you to say goodbye." He met her gaze, his voice calm and collected. "You have my word." *Believe me. Please, believe me.*

"But you're still planning on leaving." Her jaw set as she spoke. "You've got a ship waiting for you. We both know that. It could be in a day or three days, I don't know, but you'll still leave."

"I'll have to sooner or later." He didn't turn away from her, which was a start. "I don't have a ship waiting for me, not in the way you mean. I'm a captain now, with a crew and responsibilities to my crew. But – but you could come with me. There'd be a place for you on my ship. All you have to do is say the word, and we'll make it happen."

"You'd make a place for me as what, the Captain's plaything?" A glimmer of a smile flickered across her lips before it vanished and she sighed. "No, I think not. I've a job here, commitments of my own, and I'm not about to walk out on those. Whatever this is we still have between us isn't going to be permanent, is it?"

His brow creased, gaze narrowing. She was right, but it didn't feel right. He wanted to be in her life. Not for a few hours, or days, or weeks, but for the rest of his life. Their lives. "No, I suppose it isn't. Shit. I thought we could find a way around all of this. A plan which would work for both of us."

"The answer's simple, David, you don't want to admit it. We enjoy this, whatever it is, then you sign the papers to legally free us both. If down the line, we wish to continue our occasional rendezvous, then that's what we do." She pressed the matter.

"And if I want more?" He cupped her jaw, rubbing along the length of her chin with one thumb. He wanted more. So much more and she knew it. He couldn't, he wouldn't walk away from this. From her. "If we want more than this one time or a few meetings when we have the time in between everything else we're committed to doing?"

Corina shook her head, her voice thick. "No, David, you're not thinking this through. You won't surrender your position as a Captain, and I'm not going to walk out on my career. Fine, you're right, occasional meetings won't work for either of us, not with how we tend to react if others try to move in on what, or who, we consider to be ours." She swallowed hard, taking a deep breath before she continued. "This is all there is, all there can be. The sooner you accept this, the easier it will be between us."

The easier it would be for her to shut the door when he walked out of her life once more.

Chapter Five

This wasn't how he'd hoped the conversation would go when he'd walked into her quarters. He'd envisioned a session of wild, passionate sex, followed by her agreeing to hand in her papers, then they'd…

We'd do what, fly off into the never never? Reality check, please. She's already said no to joining me on my ship. Not that I can blame her. What exactly would she do if she joined me? She hasn't taken the same oath, and she might have a problem with the work we do. Fuck, she doesn't know what I do for a living. I haven't had the fucking chance to tell her.

Not entirely true. He hadn't found the time to tell her.

She hadn't tried to move away from him this time, as his erect cock reminded him. Her lips were softly parted, her eyes wide and glistening as he glanced down into them. He bit back a growl as his hands tightened on her arms as he pulled her in close, relishing the warmth of her sweetly curved body. If all they had was the here and now, then he'd take it, and the future be damned.

"David?"

"No more talking." If she told him to stop then maybe, he'd find the strength to listen. He liked to think he would. He claimed her lips, his tongue parting them with a harsh, deep thrust. Fuck, he needed this. He'd been dying to taste her since the first moment he'd laid eyes on her.

Corina moaned beneath him, her own hands fisting in the air before they found purchase on his body. Heat forged a path down into his balls, tightening them, his cock hard and thick as it pressed against his pants. This was the woman he remembered. The one who had haunted his dreams in the time they'd been apart.

He loosened his grip on her arms, breaking the kiss, and pushed her back toward the bed.

She glanced back over her shoulder and nodded. "Yes."

Last Name

He cupped one breast, running his thumb over her hard
nipple. She arched beneath his touch and stumbled the last
few steps onto the bed. As one they fell onto the soft mattress,
scattering the two pillows onto the floor. Her thighs parted
beneath him, hips lifted, rolling against his tented pants.

Clothing, they were wearing too much clothing. For a moment
he forgot how to undo his pants and debated ripping them off
before the logical part of his mind regained control long enough
to open them and shuck them off. It didn't solve the problem of
Corina's clothing.

He glanced down at her and frowned. She still wore the same
outfit she'd been wearing in the gym. Bra and sports shorts which
left her well and truly revealed to his eager, hungry gaze yet it
was still too much right now. It was a problem quickly solved. He
reached down to where he'd kicked his pants and grabbed the
knife from its sheath.

Corina's eyes widened at the sight of the blade. "What...no..."

"Shhh," he twirled the knife in his hand. "Trust me. I'd never
hurt you like that."

Her gaze flickered from the blade to his face and back again.
Not fear, not entirely, but there was a glimmer of it, and it only
added to the desire which threatened to consume him. "David. I
can't..."

"Don't move." He eased the tip between her breasts, teasing
at the cloth. He wouldn't cut her, but the idea of reducing her
clothing to shreds appealed to him. "Unless you want to be cut,
my sweet wife."

Her jaw set instantly. "You wouldn't dare."

"The wrong thing to say to me, love, as you should know." He
sliced through the cloth with a single tug. The fabric parted, baring
the full curves of her breasts, her nipples hard and ready to be
touched. He traced the tip of his tongue across his lips, his gaze
settling on them for a moment longer before he slid the blade
down to the waistband of her shorts.

Fuck. I need this. I've missed this.

She hissed, tensing beneath the passage of the blade. Fury danced in her eyes. Her arousal hadn't dimmed, but the anger had grown.

"I assumed you'd enjoy this Corina," he set the blade down on his pants and claimed her lips for a fresh kiss.

She squirmed beneath him, wriggling until she managed to press her feet against the bed. She twisted without warning, flipping them over. The bed wasn't wide enough to take it and tipped them both to the floor.

The blow knocked the wind from them bot but left Corina straddling him. For a moment he lay still, then his cock twitched against her inner thigh. "This wasn't exactly what I had in mind, but it works."

Corina arched her back, grinding her hips down against him, only a thin piece of cloth between them. Material which did nothing to hide the heat pulsing between her thighs. "I don't like knives being used like that, David. Not anymore. They're weapons, not toys."

And that's why you're damned turned on I can taste it in the air. I know you, my fierce warrior, I know yo, and the way your body reacts to me.

Denial, fear, uncertainty, he'd conquer those things in her again. He needed time, and he didn't have any to spare.

"Are you listening?"

"Got it." Right, he wouldn't use a knife again with her until she was willing to accept it was the fear of arousal that was the problem, not the blade itself. Still, it had partially stripped her, and he wasn't going to complain about the view he now enjoyed. He reached up, cupping both of her breasts, his fingers teasing across her nipples.

She whimpered, her eyes closing, hips grinding down once more as she surrendered to his touch. "Oh, fuck..."

"We'll get to that." He promised, tugging on both nipples,

rolling them between his fingers. "Soon."

"Now." She eased her hands down to her waist, undoing the shorts as she rose, pulling free of his grasp on her nipples. A hiss of pain passed through her lips as her body flushed with pleasure. Yes, she hadn't changed. Pain and pleasure, pleasure, and pain, she needed both to find a moment of release.

And he was the man to give it to her.

The shorts joined his pants on the floor, and he grinned, reaching for her hips. "Mount me."

She laughed, her hair teasing around her shoulders as she shifted her position until her core hovered above his erect cock. "Giving up control already?" She growled the words out as she pressed down, taking him into her body. "I'm surprised. It's not like you at all."

"Not bloody likely." His fingers tightened on her hips, holding her in place. Her slick inner walls clenched on his cock and he bit back a groan of delight. "Enjoying what you have to offer, my love."

"Stop calling me that. This isn't about love or marriage. Just sex." She rolled her hips, pressing down on him. Her body tight and eager around his cock. "Understand this is nothing more than sex shared by two adults, a moment to enjoy before we pass out then slip out of each other's lives."

Yes, he understood the theory, but his heart had another idea. He wanted more. He needed more than sex with her. But he knew better than to say anything to her right now. It would spoil the moment. Ruin everything between them, and there wasn't much left he could risk destroying.

"Just sex." He forced the words out as he rolled his hips, thrusting into her welcoming body. *There'd be time for more later, it's the only way this would work.* "Agreed."

She groaned, arching above him. Her full breasts lifted, nipples tight buds, her hips thrust forward as she rocked back and forth. Each movement left him struggling for control. Her tight inner walls wrapped and clenched around his cock. Her body welcoming his presence with a liquid heat threatened to consume his sanity.

Sanity is overrated, especially around Corina.

"Yes, that's it. Move for me. Dance for me. Show me the woman I remember." He growled, his fingers tight enough he knew they'd leave bruises. "Gods, I've missed you. Missed you more than I believed possible. You're in my blood, Corina. You've always been with me."

She tensed, going still for a moment. A moment he didn't enjoy. What was wrong with him telling the truth? He had missed her and missed this shared passion.

She was overthinking instead of enjoying the moment. He could take care of the problem easily enough. David lifted one hand only to bring it down against her buttocks with a loud crack. She cried out, her inner walls clenching hard and fast on his cock.

She sobbed, her eyes wide as she looked down at him. "What was that for?"

"To the victor belong the spoils." He slapped her ass again. "Dance."

Her thighs tensed. She could have moved, lifted away from him. Told him to stop. Yet she didn't. She stared down at him, her body still wrapped around his cock.

The next slap had the desired effect. His hand had barely touched her skin when she jolted, her pussy tight around his erection he could have sworn it was another hand. His balls tightened, pressing against the base of his cock. He had to keep control, and he wasn't ready to let this happen.

Corina closed her eyes once more with a soft, low moan and tossed her head back, shuddering.

"Yes, keep moving for me." He growled, tracing light fingers over the heated pattern; his spanks had left on her skin.

Beautiful. He'd never seen her this beautiful not when they'd first been together. She'd matured in those three years, become more confident and sensual, and now he could delight in those changes.

He arched, pressing his feet to the floor, lifting his hips to drive further into her clenching heat. His gaze focused on the sight of her slick folds parted around his cock. The small, ripe bud he knew was her clit, peeked out with each new roll of her hips.

"I can't hold on." Her cry echoed through the small room.

"Then don't." But he would. He had plans which wouldn't end with Corina's first orgasm. They had hours, perhaps longer if he could persuade her to take a few days off. He frowned for a moment, trying to recall what had been said in the office. Her soft cries pushed all thought to the back of his mind.

She arched, flinging her head back. Her stomach tightened, muscles taut beneath her soft skin.

"Yes. Give it to me." He cupped both her breasts, urging her on. This is what they both needed. This release, this time together where the arguments didn't matter. Where the pain was forgotten. "Let yourself go, love."

She cried out, clamped around his cock, across his hips, a thing of beauty and passion he couldn't tear his gaze from.

How he prevented himself from coming, he would never know. But somehow he kept control over his body so that when she semi-collapsed across him, he was waiting, ready to cradle her close to his chest.

Corina gasped, shuddering in his arms as she lay. Sweat beaded across her body, her inner walls rocked by spasms threatened to send her over the edge again. Her body was torn between the need to curl up and sleep, sated from what he had done and pushed for more, to drive her to the brink over and over again until she collapsed into blissful darkness.

I shouldn't have let this happen. This was wrong. He'll expect more. Oh, gods, how am I going to get him out of my system? What am I supposed to do now? Oh fuck, I shouldn't have let him touch me. Now he'll think what we had is now back to the way it was. It can't be that way again.

Her body wanted more though, and her heart was quickly following suit.

I shouldn't have done this.

But she had, and she couldn't undo it now. Nor did she want to if she was going, to be honest about the situation. Shit, she'd enjoyed it. If it meant a few sleepless nights once he left the station, then so be it. She'd find a way to deal with it.

"I think you needed that." He stroked one hand through her hair, fisting for a moment before he let go. "I should be pleased about it, but a part of me can't help but be disappointed."

"Sorry?" She frowned, searching his gaze to try and understand what he was talking about.

"Pleased you haven't found a lover to satisfy you the way I can. Disappointed you'd settle for a partner who didn't answer your desires."

Corina growled and rolled away from him, coming to her feet in one smooth move. "What the fuck – you arrogant son of a bitch. Is everything about you? Do you never think of anything except yourself?" She glared down at him, her fingers itching with the need to slap him.

How dare he. He has no right. No fucking right.

"What did I do wrong?" He frowned, sitting up. "I didn't –"

"Who I fuck, if I fuck anyone, and their skills, are none of your concern. They stopped being your concern when you walked out on me." What did he think he was doing? She didn't belong to him. She wasn't with him. This was her damned life. It didn't matter if she screwed the entire complement of the station, it had nothing to do with him.

"Excuse me?" His gaze narrowed. "You're my wife. Who you fuck, if anyone, is entirely my concern. We are, as you took the trouble to tell me, married. That makes you mine, as I'm yours."

"Mine? Yours? Are you fucking serious? You think you can

claim me? Not in this reality." Corina stalked over to the bed and grabbed her robe, tugging it on. "This is insane. You walk back into my life. We have sex. And you think you suddenly have a say in what I do? I made this clear. What we did was nothing more sex. It can't be anything more. Don't you get that?"

No, not just sex. Not according to her heart or the not so quiet voice in the back of her mind. There was more between them, she couldn't tell him. Couldn't let him know the weakness he'd uncovered or the hope which had blossomed into life, she couldn't give him power over her.

Not this time.

"Sex. Fine. Then what does that make you if you're not my wife? Are you in the habit of falling into bed with any male who walks into your life, or your rooms? Is this the woman you've become, Corina?"

Oh no. He didn't...

"Answer me, Corina. Is this the type of woman you've become?"

Heat flushed across her cheeks. "Don't fucking go there." Her hands clenched, jaw tight as she took a step toward him. "You have no damned right." If he pushed anymore, she'd punch his fucking teeth out.

"Damnit, Corina, this isn't how I planned on things working out between us." He sighed and made no attempt to reach for his pants. "I shouldn't have said — I'm sorry. I was wrong. I didn't mean you were the type to — not that it would matter if you did — fuck it, I'm not making myself explicitly clear."

She frowned, staring at his crotch and his still erect cock. He hadn't finished. It didn't make sense. Why have sex with her if he had no intention of enjoying it himself?

No, he'd enjoyed it, but why was he still erect? Why hadn't he come? Had she made a mistake? Had he lost interest in her?

No, it didn't work that way. He wouldn't have been able to get it up if he'd lost interest. What the fuck had happened?

"You're staring, what's wrong?"

"You're still hard." She kept her voice calm. "I don't get it. Didn't you enjoy what we – shit, you didn't did you?" Fantastic, absolutely bloody wonderful. She couldn't get a man to come anymore. Talk about a blow to the ego.

"No, fuck no, it's nothing like that." He pushed to his feet and cleared the distance between them. "I didn't want it to be over quickly, that's all. I'd hoped we'd have time for more."

Her throat tightened. He'd prevented himself from reaching an orgasm simply because he hadn't wanted it to be a quickie? "I see." She didn't know what else to say to him. She couldn't stay angry with him, not with that piece of information. Nor did she want him to stay in the room with her.

"Shit, I'm sorry, Corina. I didn't mean to push things. The idea of you with another is enough to make my blood boil. I still- -"

"Still what, love me? You don't love me. If you did, you'd have come searching for me long before this. You can throw a dozen excuses at me for why you didn't, but love would have found a way." She couldn't raise the energy required to shout at him. "I think it would be best if you get dressed and leave. I don't think I can do this right now." Or ever if she had her way. The faster she got him out of her quarters and her life, the easier it would be to cope.

His jaw set. "No, I don't think so. We haven't finished our talk. I'm not leaving until we've got all of this sorted out, Corina."

Talk? It was one word for what they'd been doing, but it wasn't what she'd call it. Her gaze slipped down to take in his naked cock, his shirt still in place, but it wasn't long enough to cover his groin. Then she forced herself to meet his gaze once more. "I don't believe I was giving you a choice, David. I'm telling you to leave before I call security. I'm not kidding this time. I don't care what happens, I'll get you out of here one way or another."

Yes, and how's that going to look if they turn up, find me naked or semi-naked, smelling of sex, with a naked man in my quarters, demanding he leave? Shit, I'll never live this one down.

He moved toward her, his shoulders set. "I won our fight, remember? We had an agreement about what would happen if I won the fight."

"Yes, I remember, but you've had your fun." She stared, pointedly, at his groin. "It's time to leave."

"Not entirely," he growled. "As you noted yourself, I haven't finished, and part of the arrangement remains incomplete."

Her heart skipped a beat as her inner walls clenched. His growl, his glare, the way he moved toward her, it all combined to tell her he wasn't about to back down. And there was a part of her, a large part, which liked that about him.

His strength, his willingness to stand up to her when she was wrong, or not being fair, had been one of the things she'd been drawn to from the beginning. Now the same strength stared her in the face. "Sign the papers. Now."

"No."

She hadn't expected him to say anything else. "David, we'd be better discussing things when we were calmer. Instead of fighting, pushing at each other like this. We're not in the right frame of mind to --"

"To what? To do this?" He reached out, tangling his fingers in her hair before he pulled her close, her body pressed tight against his.

She could have fought, called out or slammed a knee into his groin, but she did none of these things. She didn't have it in her to hurt him anymore. He didn't kiss her, but this time she reached up and pulled his lips down to meet hers. Her tongue parted his lips, delving into the warmth she knew well.

She needed this and wasn't about to back away. If he wasn't going to leave, then she'd take full control of the situation.

The heat from the spanking still tingled across her skin, though she tried to fight it, to ignore its presence. She wasn't going to be submissive to him anymore. She shouldn't have let the submissive streak hit her in the first place though she could admit if only to herself, it was right with him. Outside, to others, she had to keep up the walls, and with them, she was stronger than that. She had a job, a career, a plan for the rest of her life and she was respected as a strong, confident, warrior woman in the service of the peacekeepers.

But she couldn't deny her submissive side, at least to him, was a natural part of who she was.

His fingers tightened in her hair as their tongues danced, fighting for control of the kiss. A fight she lost. He growled against her lips, his teeth grazing her bottom lip, stealing her breath as she tried to pull away.

Her hips rolled, pressing against his cock, his grip tight in her hair that small shards of pain danced across her scalp. She moaned into the kiss, giving up on the fight, softening beneath him as a part of her cried out in protest. Tears stung at in her eyes, threatening to spill down her cheeks but she blinked them back.

Please more. Don't stop. Don't leave me hanging.

"No need to cry, love." He brushed his free hand over her hair then down to her cheek, cupping her chin. "I can see the tears in your eyes, don't deny it. I know I've hurt you. I hurt both of us with what I had to do. But I had no choice, I had to follow orders. You understand how it works. If they give you an order, you follow through, or you quit the service. No third option, not normally at least."

She opened her mouth to speak, but he pressed a finger to her lips. Leaning against him, using his strength as a means to recover, would have been easy, but she wasn't going to make that mistake. Not this time. She could deal with this on her own as she had when he'd walked out on her.

"No, please, let me finish love. I should have come for you. I should have contacted you. I was wrong, how I handled all of this was wrong and cruel." He took a deep breath and rolled his shoulders back, lifting his head until he met her gaze head-on once more. "What I did threatened to destroy me, and what it did to you I can only imagine. I convinced myself I could handle leaving you, but once I'd left it hit me. For the past three years, there's been a piece missing from my life, and now I know it's you. For all this and much more, I'm sorry. I can only hope you believe me and accept what I'm saying as the truth. I never meant to hurt you."

Gods how she wanted to believe him. For a moment she closed her eyes and leaned into his touch, remembering other times, places, the joy they'd shared, but much had changed in the time they'd been apart. She was no longer willing to turn her back on her career. And he was a ship's captain with all the responsibilities which came with such a position.

"I do accept it." She whispered, the tight bands around her heart loosening at her own words. "But you have to accept things have changed. We're not the same people we were three years ago. Shit, I don't know where the real you starts, and your cover story begins. All the stories about your family, your brother, the plans and dreams you had for your life, for our lives together, as far as I now know they were all a lie. I can't live with that hanging over me and accept you as a part of my life again." She took a deep breath and forced herself to keep calm. "How much of what you told me was real, David? How much was real, I need to know. You have to tell me what was the truth and what was a lie designed to lure me in."

She had to know all the gory details. Everything she'd built the dream on now needed to be torn apart and examined before she could deal with it all. If he didn't tell her right away, then she'd push until he did.

I'm doing the right thing, aren't I?

"David, I need to know."

"Most of it was the truth." His voice low as he dropped his hand away from her face. "I had to lie, to protect others and I swear I'll tell you the truth of who and what I am. But what I told you about how I felt, how I still feel, wasn't a lie. Nor is the fact I have a brother. Those weren't lies. I can't ask you to turn back the clock, to become the woman you were, but will ask this much. Give me a chance to get to know you again."

Get to know her again? Why did he want to get to know her anyway if he was leaving again in a couple of days?

"Corina?"

"I need a moment to think about this." She stepped out of the circle of his embrace. Time. Did they have the time to do this? "When are you leaving the station? I need a serious answer here, if you don't know for certain, don't lie. It will only make matters worse in the long run."

He paused for a moment, his gaze narrowing. "Three days. Maybe four or five if things work out. A lot depends on when the next orders come in."

"Not long then." But was it long enough? Who was he getting his orders from? He'd sworn he'd tell her the truth, but when?

Long enough for what?

"No, as I said, I didn't know you were here." He didn't move, his gaze locked on her face. "I'm due out in system three for a few months. Then I'll have a month off. Unless something comes up. Duty. A change in orders. You know what it's like."

"Yeah, I do." She rubbed the back of her neck, thinking. What did she have to lose? She did know what it was like to be under orders and follow through with orders she disagreed with so why shouldn't she give him a chance? "All right, then I'll give you those three days but not a moment longer, but I want a promise from you. If they tell you that you're leaving sooner than planned for, you come and find me. You tell me what's going on this time. I still don't get what's going on with you, but I'm trusting you to follow through with your word. You will explain to me what's going on here."

"I'll do my best, but I can't give you a promise. Not right now at least but thank you for agreeing to the extra time. You won't regret it. And I'll find the time to explain to you what's been going on. You're right, you need answers, deserve answers, and I'm not going to lie to you this time."

A part of her already did regret it – she regretted opening the door a crack, but there was no going back now. She needed answers, needed to know if this could work. She had to even if it tore her apart. "I hope not." She looked back at him. "But, I think you should go, for now, I mean." As much as she needed to know, she also needed space, time to think, and put the need to comply, submit to him, under control. This submissive side to her nature wasn't one she had time for now, nor did he need to know how close she'd come to losing control of the situation.

He frowned, uncertain if she meant it. "Why?"

"You've walked back into my life, and things have changed. We both need time to get used to it." *Please, don't ask too many questions. Don't remember how I reacted to your control.*

"But I- -"

"No, I'm not backing down, not this time. Please, get dressed and leave. We'll finish this – whatever it is – later." Perhaps it wasn't fair to him, but it was the best she could offer right now. It wasn't that she didn't want him. She did. After her orgasm, she was ready for round two. Or rather her body was. Her mind, however, was another matter entirely, and she didn't want to get into what her heart was telling her.

"Okay, I don't like it, but I'll accept it. But I'll be back in two hours."

"Five." Corina folded her arms beneath her breasts. "I need at least five hours."

"Two. If all I have is three days, then I'm not going to wait around for half a day so you can get your mind in order."

Corina growled, shaking her head. "Stop pushing things, David. Five hours isn't half a day, not a quarter of a day. You've already pissed me off several times in the past couple of hours, and your lousy math isn't helping the situation."

"I'm giving you the two hours, but that's it." He stopped down, grabbing his pants. "Then I'm coming back, and we're going to grab a meal."

"Pardon?" As in go out and have a meal together? Was he insane? There would be other people around who would see them together then she'd have a dozen questions from people who claimed to be her friends.

"We started off the wrong way the first time around, just sex, sex, marriage, sex, and then I left. I don't want to make the same mistake this time. I'm going to get to know you this time. Shit, for all I know, we won't be able to stand each other outside of sex."

For a moment, she knee-jerked then stopped, took a deep breath, and let his words sink in. Not like each other? *And why am I upset by the idea?* Besides, he wasn't saying sex was a mistake, not getting to know her, all of her, had been the mistake. And he was right.

Maybe they could make this work. At least the early stages of it.

Hope fluttered into life in her breast, and she took a long, deep, slow breath, forcing herself to calm down. This wasn't a matter to rush into, yet she couldn't turn away from this option he was offering her. Not if it gave her a chance, however small, to be happy.

"Okay, two hours, dinner, and then we talk. Somewhere public, where we won't be tempted to make a mistake." Tempted. Oh, they'd be tempted. She'd be tempted. It was taking all of her self-control not to tumble him into the bed again. Safe. She was safe with him when sex was involved but at all other times – they'd been strangers.

She met his gaze, her heart threatening to pound its way out of her chest. What the hell was going on here? She wasn't in love with him, not anymore.

Then why was she now acting as if this was her first date? *Because it is, at least with him.*

Chapter Six

David took a deep breath and leaned against the wall two corridors away from Corina's room, trying to put his mind into order. Two men in station uniforms walked past, barely glancing at him, and he wanted to shut them out of his thoughts. There was no place for anyone else right now. Not his crew. Corina consumed him.

The woman certainly knew how to leave him unsettled, but she'd always had that type of effect on him. Still, this wasn't, exactly, how he'd hoped things would turn out, but this was better. She'd given him a chance to work things out between them.

A chance I don't deserve if the truth be told. Not after the way things ended last time.

He'd screwed up her life, if she was to be believed, beyond all expectations. Left her in a situation where she'd had to figure out what was going on, with no one to help her figure it all out. He wanted to turn and knock on her door again to find out exactly what had happened when he'd left her on Fartier Station, but the sane part of his mind reminded him what a terrible idea it would be, especially when she'd agreed to give him a chance.

Above all, this meant he had the chance to change her mind or come to terms with whatever it was that still existed between them. She couldn't deny there was a connection, a compelling need, a tug clawed at them, forcing them to confront each other. It wasn't about to die because he'd been missing from her life.

Shit, he hadn't bedded another woman since they'd parted ways. He'd had plenty of opportunities, yet he hadn't done a damn thing about it. Odd, he hadn't thought about how little interest he'd had in women after meeting Corina. When it had crossed his mind, he'd put it down to the pressures of work. Now he knew better.

Except she's unlikely to let the matter rest and she has the right to beat me to a pulp over all of this.

Fair point, she was both a woman and peacekeeper. Both meant she'd ask questions, and if he wanted to build anything between them, he would have to tell her the truth. The entire truth. No matter how it made him appear.

Yeah, and how am I going to explain it to the higher-ups? How can I balance all of this? My oath and the woman I want to spend the rest of my life with?

No one had ever told him it was going to be easy. He was going to do it regardless. He glanced back in the direction of her quarters before he tucked in his shirt and headed for the docking ring. At least he'd be able to clean up and check in on things before he met up with Corina again. The joys of being a ship's Captain.

Not that he'd turn his back on the ship, or its crew, not even for Corina. He'd worked too hard to get where he was now. It wasn't a part of his nature.

Except maybe it is.

He faltered, pausing in the corridor. Would he give it all up for her? Could he turn in his papers and walk away from the Shadow Rangers? Fuck, the idea was one to think about. He couldn't tell Corina who he worked for, despite the fact the Shadow Rangers and the peacekeepers were technically on the same side.

Except when they're not. That had happened more than a time or two and would no doubt occur in the future. It was the way the situation occasionally worked out. Trouble is when they went head to head, things tended to become messy.

Very few people knew the Rangers officially existed. They worked out of the way, undercover, or however, else you wanted to describe it. He knew only a few members of the Rangers outside of those on his ship, and maybe three or four people had access to the names of each man and woman who had signed up.

He hadn't regretted signing with them until Corina. Then he'd managed to push it all to the back of his mind until he'd seen

Last Name

Corina again. It was one of the reasons the Rangers preferred to either take on married teams or single operatives. The married teams were rare and thoroughly vetted to make sure they were a stable unit who couldn't be turned on each other.

Not too many of those around.

Now there was a depressing idea. He sighed and looked back at Corina's door. A woman he could trust, but telling her who he worked for could never happen, no matter how much he may wish it could be otherwise.

Perhaps this once?

No, it wasn't possible. Besides, it was the woman who was supposed to step back from his career, or family, or whatever they had to hold them to a place.

It wasn't worth thinking about. No, she'd come around. She'd realize she couldn't stay on the station and they'd find a way to work it all out. Perhaps she could be persuaded to join the Rangers – which would mean explaining to her what he did and answering all of the questions which would follow. It wasn't the best of answers, but it was still workable, and she'd be happy with him...

Like hell, she would. She's worked too hard to walk away from it all now.

Right, he knew better. She'd never walk out on her work, and he'd have thought less of her if she did. He shook his head and tried to turn his mind away from Corina, at least for the time being.

He hid his emotions behind a mask of calm before he keyed in the entrance code to his ship. He couldn't risk letting anyone see what he was dealing with right now. That would lead to far too many questions. Better to wait until he knew what was going on before he faced the rest of the crew.

"Captain?"

The female voice drew his attention instantly as he stepped onto his ship. "Yes, Amber?"

"We've got messages from command waiting for you." The tall, leggy brunette stepped to one side before she matched his pace into the depths of the vessel. The competent woman had become a valuable member of his crew over the time she'd served with him, and he was grateful she was the one who had come to meet him when he'd returned to the ship.

"How bad is it?" Work. He could focus on work and deal with the rest later.

"Your eyes only, Captain. Encoded." The woman replied calmly. "Highest priority, Captain."

Shit. Encoded was never good. "When did they arrive, Amber?" Why now when he finally had a chance to fix things with Corina?

Because Murphy was an optimist and I'm personal friends with his evil twin Skippy.

"First one an hour ago, the second arrived five minutes ago," Amber explained in a calm voice as they made their way to his quarters. "We tried to contact you, but you had privacy mode switched on your com." She nodded toward the small silver item attached to David's belt. "I attempted to buzz through, but you'd switched to your other codes, and I don't have the rating to break through on those."

No, she wouldn't. Only Blain and one other would be able to do that. Essential but not the end of the universe, and they were all about to die.

"Ah, I forgot to – well – never mind." No, he hadn't forgotten. He'd turned off everything for the fight and left it that way. He'd wanted to be left alone while he dealt with Corina and had hoped he could have the time he had needed. Obviously, it had been a mistake.

"Understood, Captain."

He sighed and fixed the setting on his com. "Fine, I'll see to whatever they've sent me, and we'll go from there." If this meant leaving the station, he'd have to explain it all to Corina.

Last Name

And shit, wouldn't she love that one. He finally had a chance to patch things up with her, and it had all been blown to hell in a handbasket in a few hours.

Skippy, I'm coming to find you, and when I do it won't be pretty, you better run while you still have the chance. I mean it this time. I'm going to hunt you down if it's the last damn thing I do.

Amber smiled and waited patiently at the side of the door. "I'll be here if you need me, Captain." She smiled and rested one hand on her hip. The grey and blue one-piece uniform clung in all the right places, and if it hadn't been for Corina, the pose would have sent a jolt of arousal through his body.

Odd, when he'd believed he'd never see Corina again, he'd been unaffected by Amber, and it was only now he had begun to realize the level of power Corina had over him. Gods, what was he getting himself into with Corina? Why couldn't he remember a time, after meeting her, when he'd been attracted to another woman?

Because you were always in love with Corina. The sooner you admit it, the easier it will be for all concerned.

It was old news. No point in wasting more time thinking that one through.

David double checked the seal on his door before sitting down at his console. An eyes only code wasn't used lightly, which meant the shit had hit the fan and he was supposed to fix it or get to the bottom of the situation. Exactly what he'd signed up for many years ago and until he turned in his papers, this would remain his priority in life.

He punched in his code then let the console scan his DNA before he was able to lean back and wait for the first of the messages to play.

A salt and pepper haired man with steel grey eyes appeared on the small holoprojector pad. Blain. His hands were folded behind his back, his jaw set. "Captain Monroe, there will be a prisoner exchange taking place on Freedom Station in two days.

However, it's imperative one of the prisoners, Drake Aspenwing, isn't handed over to the Mensarans." The holographic man smiled slightly, the first giveaway this wasn't a recording but a live connection. Sneaky.

Mensarans, the women who ruled the planet Mensara, and handing over a male prisoner to them wasn't ideal under the best of circomestances. If the man was an escaped male or had committed a crime under Mensaran law, then his death was all but confirmed.

The arena wasn't a fate he'd wish on his worst enemy.

Drake Aspenwing? Where had he come across that name before? He scowled, trying to put the pieces together. Fuck, he hated it when his mind refused to spit out the information on command. Fine. The Mensarans wouldn't treat a male prisoner with consideration, as their counterparts the Mensarians, would enslave and mistreat any female prisoner they laid their hands upon. If he lived long enough to make it to the games, then he'd face a short, painful life, fighting daily until he finally left this life with his blood spilled on the sands of the arena.

"The hand over will place this Drake in a situation no man deserves. I won't ask what crime he committed for this to be his fate, as I presume you want me to help get him out, sir." Which might be doable but it wouldn't be easy. "I've got a few friends here, which could be useful."

"Indeed and as such, we need you to use your unique connections with the peacekeepers of Freedom Station to take control of Drake and bring him in."

Shit.

"Further details to follow." The connection ended with the holograph flickering out as he watched.

What the hell was going on here? When had Drake been taken, and why would anyone hand him over to the Mensarans? Where the Mensarians involved in this mess? The peacekeepers wouldn't like being drawn into all of this, but they had to abide by the terms of the treaties.

He frowned and shifted to the second message, going through the security checks again before the message would play. This time the figure was a younger man, one he knew all too well.

"Hey, bro. Don't ask me how I got this one smuggled out, you don't want to know. But hey, we can catch up after you spring me, right?" A recorded message with no chance he could reply, but it was the man in the recording who made the difference. The face, like his own, flickered out of existence and David blinked. His brother. Drake Aspenwing was his brother's cover.

Fuck. What the hell is going on here? Hey, Skippy, don't pull this because I've found Corina again. I don't deserve this shit.

How could he pull this off without blowing his friendship with Kraven or destroying what he had with Corina? Of all the things which could have gone wrong, could have turned things upside down, this was the worst. What the hell was he supposed to do now?

Refuse the mission.

Not an option. He was still oath-bound, and though it was a different branch, technically, of the Peacekeepers, Corina and Kraven would want his hide if he went through with this.

If?

Okay, there was no if, not knowing who Drake was. Turning him over to the Mensarans was problematic to begin with, which begged the question – who the hell had him now?

David Monroe. Ever since that delicious, arrogant asshole had walked into her life, she'd dealt with one problem after another, but this was more than she could handle.

Corina sighed and held up another dress in front of the mirror. What was she doing with this? The dress wasn't her. She sighed and tossed it on the pile before picking up the next one only to shudder before she dropped it.

"This isn't going to work. None of these are right."

"Try the red with the silver trim," Jana suggested from the chair in the changing room. "That one with a pair of *do me* heels would turn any male to mush. You have to try them on. Come on, for me if no one else."

"Do what heels? What are you talking about?" Corina glanced back over her shoulder and scowled at the pair of impossible heels Jana held up. Did people actually wear those things without breaking their necks? "No way. Not fucking happening. I'm not going to kill myself by wearing break my neck heels. They're ridiculous. How the hell do you walk in those things?"

"Corina, come on, with your legs you'd be amazing in these." She dangled the shoes by the tiny straps and grinned. "Maybe you'd need to practice walking in those things first, but once you got the hang of it, you'd knock him dead. Please. You have to let me see you wear these." Jana batted her eyelashes and grinned.

"Not happening." Why was she doing this in the first place? She didn't do dresses, heals, do me shoes, or anything else. She wore clothes she could fight in or move in, not clothes to tempt a man. "This is insane. I don't need to buy a damned dress to meet him for a simple drink." She didn't own any dresses, why would she need to change to meet David?

"Because you're going on a date. The first date I've ever known you to agree to, and you have to do it the right way." Jana sighed and put the heels down. "Didn't your mother teach you about these things? No, never mind, I guess not. Okay, you're supposed to make an effort, dress up, go all girly on him. You do understand what I mean by girly, right? I mean you're a woman, and I know you're part Gaean, so you've got to understand what it all means. You gotta work those hips until he falls at your feet begging to kiss your heels or whatever you're going to wear."

"Yes, of course, I know what going all girly means, but it doesn't mean I'm willing to turn into a woman I'm not." Corina hung the dress back up and turned to leave the changing room.

Last Name

"Not for David."

"You can't mean to go to meet this David of yours in your normal get up?" Jana followed her out of the small room. "Not a different set of shoes, or a top? Corina, you're letting the side down. Please, at least try for me."

There was a side? She must have missed the lecture on that one – right along with shutting out the speeches on sexuality, being feminine, drawing in a man and every other one her mother had tried to drum into her. Still, sides. It was a new one from Jana. "I don't get it, that's all. Why I have to dress up to meet a man instead of being myself." He already knew what she looked like, didn't he? Besides, she wasn't her mother with a different outfit for each possible mood or situation. Such fripperies didn't interest her at all.

Jana laughed, and the sound stopped Corina in her tracks. "What is it?"

"I love you like a sister, but there are times you can be so naïve it frightens me." Jana rested one hand on Corina's arm. "Be yourself, be comfortable, but try. Men normally make an effort when they're on a date. It might be an idea to offer him the same courtesy in return. Besides, you might find you like doing it."

Corina couldn't believe it. No, David would have to be satisfied with how she was, not all prettified for his amusement. "I can't go through with it. Besides, I'd fall over in those things." She gestured at the heels.

"Who is he? This man you're meeting?" Jana dumped the heels back with the others. "I mean, I know his name is David, but I don't know anything about him. He's not a resi here, is he? Which ship does he serve on, or is he a new rotation?"

"Captain Monroe." No point hiding it. "I don't know the name of his ship, but he's an independent Captain." Independent Captain. How many times had that been another name for pirate, or runner, or worse? What the hell was he doing anyway? It was yet another question she needed an answer to, especially as he claimed he had other people he answered to.

Orders which had separated them three years ago.

"Monroe?" Jana walked alongside of Corina in silence for several long minutes as they left the shopping strip, one of several in the station. "Oh, Kraven's friend? The one who arrived yesterday? Playing it fast and loose, aren't you? And a ship's Captain? How long is he staying? Oh, does he have a brother? I mean, does he have a friend I could get to know. We could double date or whatever. I've never had the chance to do that."

"We're not double dating. I'm not sure I'm up to dating." Twenty questions. She hadn't signed up for that either. "Does it matter how long he's staying?"

"Ah, okay. Then it's nothing serious between you. Pity."

No, he's my husband who I forgot to mention to the only real female friend I've ever had. Nope, not serious at all. "Exactly. Nothing serious at all. This is a drink and a chat. I doubt I'll stay for more than one drink, I've got far too many other things to deal with." As long as they stayed in public, that is all it would be. Taking it private was an entirely different matter. "I'll stop in, have a drink, then I'll be heading back to my quarters. Alone."

"And you're still off duty, right? I mean, Kraven's still pissed at you about the fight. Not that you did anything wrong either. Okay, maybe you should have called for help but –"

"Jana," Corina stopped and took in the slender woman with long, pale hair. One of her few friends on the station and – in truth – her only female friend.

"I'm babbling again, aren't I?" The younger woman sighed and pushed a loose strand of hair back from her eyes. "Sorry, I keep trying to get it under control, but then something else catches my attention, and off I go again."

Jana was a lovely soul, and Corina had come to realize it after a few days on the station. Sadly, the gentle soul made her a target for some of the visitors and the Peacekeepers, along with medical and the station's maintenance division had taken it upon themselves to act as watchdogs for the woman. Any attempt to persuade her to find a safer place to live had fallen on deaf ears. Her father had been born on the station, so had Jana and as such this was home.

Home.

When was the last time she'd called a place her home?

With David. Before he left that night. I won't make the same mistake again.

"Corina?" Jana touched her left arm, her touch light but her voice filled with concern. "You vanished on me for a minute. Are you all right? I've never seen you like this before. I mean, you actually like this guy, don't you?"

"Yeah, sorry." David did that to her way too often. An infuriating aspect of the man and his ability to worm into her mind. Shit, she had to get it under control before she met up with him. "And you're fine. The babbling is a part of who you are. I don't mind it. I'm not sure if I like him or not, but I guess it's partially what this date thing is all about." She gave a small shrug and hoped Jana would drop the subject.

"Like getting into trouble because a Mensarian thinks I'm an easy target. Yeah, I get it. And don't worry, I'm fine, they've been giving me a wide berth for the past couple of weeks. Ever since you and Kraven warned them off." Jana snaked an arm around Corina's waist and hugged. "Don't worry about me, okay? I'm fine. I'm not going to let them get to me. If I'm out of my depth, I call for help. I know the rules, and I'm not going to change. Please, don't worry about me."

"Like that's going to stop anytime soon." Corina pulled Jana in tighter. "I'll always worry about you; it's just a part of my life on this station." A life she wasn't about to walk out on, not for David or anyone else.

Damnit. I've worked too long to give it all up for a man.

Jana pulled free and moved to stand in front of Corina. "I know you all think I'm weak and need looking after. I don't take offense, but it would be nice if you guys let me learn how to take care of myself. I mean, I can handle things you know. I'm not a kid anymore, even if I act like one occasionally."

Corina blinked and stared at Jana. Where had that come from? "I don't understand…"

"I want to learn to defend myself, Corina instead of having to rely on other people stepping in to save me. I mean learn more than the scream, kick, and call for help. I don't want to spend the rest of my life leaning on other people for protection. I'm smart, I get it. I babble at time but give me a piece of machinery, and I can fix it, even if I've never seen it before. I should be smart enough to learn where to punch, kick, how to get free, and how to shoot a damned gun if need be." Jana shifted her weight from one foot to the other and back again. "All I need is a teacher patient enough to show me what to do."

Had they denied Jana the chance to be independent in all things because she was nothing more than a little girl in their eyes? Okay, that wasn't fair either. She was a grown woman with the curves to match, but there was a delicate side to her. An intense interest glowed in her eyes and showed in her face, which couldn't be denied. It's what brought out the protective streak in both her and Kraven, hell in anyone who named Jana as one of their friends.

"Never mind, forget I said anything. It's not the important thing right now; we need to focus on getting you ready for this David." Jana sighed and checked the time. "You're going to be late for your date, and I can't let that happen. Not and have it be my fault."

"He can wait, this is more important." Shit, she'd waited long enough for him, now he could return the favor. She glanced around and pulled Jana toward a small café. What had gotten into Jane; where had all this come from?

"No, he can't. He's likely not going to be here for long, and I'm not going to be the reason you avoid this date. We'll talk tomorrow, after my shift, okay?" Jana grinned and pulled her arm free for a second time. "Go back to your quarters and get ready. He's likely sent you a dozen messages already and wants to know what's going on."

"No, we're going to have this discussion now, Jana. He can and will wait. Shit, he'll be gone within a few days and I'm not turning my back on my friend for a man who comes and goes when he wants to." When Jana tried to protest, Corina held up one hand to silence her. "You'd do the same for me, and we both know it."

Jana sighed and nodded before she pulled up a chair and sat down. "Okay, fine. You're right. I would. Doesn't mean I like it though."

One argument down, a dozen more to go before the end of the day.

"Are we holding you back, Jana?"

The younger woman smiled her voice gentle. "Kinda, I know you guys mean well but any time I try to handle a situation on my own you step in to fix things, or Kraven does, instead of helping me gain the tools to fix things myself."

Corina frowned and tried to think back over the last few incidents. "We're trying to protect you, Jana. You're not a warrior and…"

"It doesn't mean I shouldn't be able to protect myself. At least enough to buy time until back up arrives. If I can't there's going to be a situation, maybe not now, maybe not for several years, where back up doesn't arrive and I'm either dead, raped, kidnapped or a combination of all of that." Jana never raised her voice, but there was a soft quiver behind the words.

Shit. If she'd missed it, Kraven should have caught it, and yet neither of them had. "Okay, okay, I can see your point. We screwed up."

"No, I did. I should have forced the issue before now."

Jana, forcing the issue? It wasn't in her nature. "We're going to fix it. I'll talk to Kraven and figure it out. Maybe a basic course in self-defense." A course they should offer to every crew member on the station now she had a chance to think about it.

These were lessons she could run, especially for the women who came to the station. She knew the moves which would work best for women of smaller stature. It made her, potentially, the best person for the job. She'd have to find time to speak to Kraven.

"You should check your com, Corina. He's going to be waiting for you by now." Jana smiled and rolled out her shoulders before she stood back up. "But thank you. Really, thank you. I needed this, needed to know there was a chance I could be more than the woman in hiding."

Corina pulled the com from her belt and winced, three unanswered messages which had to be from David. Anything work related would have come straight through on a security override and other than Jana, she couldn't think of anyone else who would call her.

Except, maybe, for Piotr or Jana, and Jana didn't count in this situation.

Her stomach knotted. A date. A real, gods be damned date. What the hell had she been thinking in agreeing to this nonsense? *Like he gave me a choice?* Okay, fair, he hadn't, but she could have found a way out of it.

"Well?"

"All right, all right, I'm going." She pulled Jana in for a quick hug before hurrying away.

Damn the man for turning her into a nervous schoolgirl and damn her for letting it happen in the first place.

Chapter Seven

David's cock throbbed as he stood under the water in the shower. His balls tightened against the base of his protesting erection, the ache deep enough that the caress of the water was almost enough to tip him over the edge and into the welcome of oblivion. He groaned and soaped himself down, carefully avoiding his cock and balls, but it didn't help. His prick demanded attention and each drop of water which touched his aching flesh added to his torment.

Oh fuck.

He couldn't meet Corina like this. If he didn't get this under control, then he'd barely be able to think around her, and the meeting was going to be hard enough as it was. The idea of masturbating sat ill with him right now, though he had no idea why what other choice did he have if he wanted to be able to handle sitting down at a table and holding a conversation with her.

Do it. She'll never know, and I'll feel better.

Maybe he would, so why couldn't he reach down and take care of the problem?

She doesn't have to know. Hell, I could imagine she's here with me. She used to enjoy watching me – she'd enjoy it again.

"What the fuck am I doing?" He closed his eyes and leaned against the wall of the shower stall. How often had he played, masturbated, in front of Corina? She'd done the same for him, using it as a form of foreplay or simply for the enjoyment of watching each other in the throes of pleasure.

Do it again. At least then I can spend time with her without shifting my cock and trying not to act like a horny teenager.

His hand closed around his erection, and he squeezed slowly, shuddering as the first waves of pleasure rippled through his body. He moved his hand slowly up and down his thick cock, stroking, bringing himself closer to the edge but despite the urge to go faster, stroke until he came, he kept the movements slow and deliberate.

He stopped for a moment and reached under, cupping his heavy sac. His balls ached with the need to be emptied, but there was a touch lacking in what he was doing. A piece only she could replace but she wasn't here, and he knew how to bring himself to release without needing a woman, physically, with him. His mind would fill in all the details he needed.

It would have been easier if she was here with him. He closed his eyes, remembering how she had been. How she had danced on him. The feel of her thighs around his, or between his, or simply pressed against him. The curve of her back, the smooth feel of her backside beneath his hand, and the way she moved with him. Oh gods, so right when he drove his cock into her body to the timing of her clenching core.

"Fuck," he hissed, stroking faster as he worked his cock in his hand.

His woman. She was his no matter how she might protest the fact. They were married. It had been done in the eyes of her people, and now he could think of no other life except one where she was at his side. At his side and in his bed for the rest of their lives.

Better yet bent over the bed, her thighs spread as he filled her. The slick sounds of their passion filling the air. Her soft cries of delight too much...

His cock pulsed in his grip and he groaned, his hips rolling, thrusting into his hand. So close, so very close, it wouldn't take much longer.

Corina, delicious, spirited Corina. The woman he belonged with, now and always. The woman he would fight to find a way to be with. She was his. He belonged to her. No avoiding it.

His balls tightened until he swore they would split. His cock hard, pulsing and eager to push its way between her thighs but all he had at this moment was his hand. His hand and his memories of how she had moved for him.

Water slipped down over his face, onto his chest, tugging at his nipples. More drops of water pulled at his sack and slid down his erection, adding to the pleasure of his own, tight grasp.

The slick, pink parted folds of her pussy, the way she bent over the bed, the scent of her arousal filling the air.

"Yes...Corina, Gods yes." he groaned between clenched teeth, his hips thrusting, pounding into his hand, his seed thick and hot spurting over his hand only to be washed away by the warm water of the shower.

He sighed and opened his eyes, taking a deep breath to bring his nerves back under control. Now he could face his woman without wanting to tear her clothes off where she sat, or at least that was the plan...

David Monroe glanced at the time for the second time and fought the urge to get up from the table to pace. How long had he been sat here? Not that it mattered, he'd been on time, and she was, of course, late.

Had he expected her to be on time? He frowned and forced himself not to recheck the time. Like a matter of seconds would have made a real difference. Shit, he didn't like this. She wasn't the type to be late – at least not the woman he had known. Anytime they'd arranged to meet before, she'd been there either early or in a few minutes of the arranged time. Work had occasionally delayed her, but she'd done the polite thing back then and let him know what was going on.

She's changed. We both have.

Yeah, and she was still late.

Oh, if this had been a shift, she'd have been ten minutes early, ready for action and no excuses would have been tolerated but for an arranged meeting with him? No, she was late, fifteen minutes so, and with no sign or message hinted at when she might arrive.

She's going to drive me to drink or worse. Gods know what I'd be like if I hadn't taken matters in hand.

Or she'd kill him when she found out what his current orders entailed. How the hell could he build the trust between them if he was going to yank a prisoner out from under her nose and do a runner before she or Kraven could stop him? No, it wasn't an option, which meant she'd find out sooner or later.

Or Kraven would.

Wonderful, either hurt a man who had been his friend for over ten years or hurt the woman he loved. Then, of course, there was the worst case scenario where he hurt and lost both of them.

Funny, twenty-four hours ago he'd have been more concerned about Kraven's reaction to the news. Now the idea of seeing the shock of betrayal on Corina's face was more than he could bear to think about. She'd have every reason to shoot him, turn him in and shoot his ass a second time to be on the safe side.

No, don't think about it. Try and enjoy the moment – when she turns up.

If she turned up.

Of course, it was, and she might have decided this wasn't worth the effort and she was simply avoiding him. If nothing else this situation had shown him how easy it was to give into self-doubt. Not a fact he enjoyed finding out about himself, and he'd find a way to bring it back under control before it tore him apart.

He'd teased and joked with men who had acted this way before, but he'd never believed he would become one of them.

A small movement caught his attention out of the corner of her eye, and his heart skipped a beat. Sure, she hadn't donned a dress, or skirt, or tried anything special, but this was his Corina. She walked with a confident stride and a slight, sexy, sway of hips which made men and women alike stop to watch her. Her shoulders were back, head held high, and the confidence which oozed from her made it clear she was ready to take on the sector if it got in her way.

He pushed to his feet and pulled out the chair opposite his, indicating she should sit down.

A small frown furrowed her brow. "I don't..."

"Let me at least play at being the gentleman for a moment or two," he sighed still holding the chair. Damn the woman for pushing on the most ridiculous of things. "Is that hard?"

"Despite the fact you're a chest-thumping barbarian and not a gentleman?" She slid into the offered seat. "Perhaps you hope I'll forget what you're like?"

His hand itched with the need to touch her, but he stepped away and settled in on the other side of the table. She was right, he was the chest thumping, throw his woman over his shoulder and stalk off, type of guy but he could give this gentleman getting to know her thing a try.

He stifled a groan as he glanced at her again. This was the wrong place for this conversation. He needed to be in a place where he could strip her naked and leave her moaning again. He wanted to pull her into his arms and claim her lips with a kiss which would leave them both panting for more, but the agreement had been a meal, not another sexual encounter. His cock thickened and pressed against his pants, his balls tight and aching, reminding him he hadn't actually come the last time they were together, and the small release in the shower wasn't going to be enough. How could it be when she looked this damned tempting? Fuck, what would he be like if he hadn't done that?

Silence enfolded the table.

What was he supposed to say? He couldn't compliment her on her outfit as she was wearing what she'd normally wear off duty. And her hair, she'd brushed it but nothing else. No make-up, no perfume, nothing out of the ordinary for Corina —how was he supposed to break the ice?

Several more minutes passed before Corina coughed and finally spoke. "Aren't we supposed to talk?"

"Yes, sorry. Your day, how was it?"

She rolled her eyes. "We've been apart two hours, well, two and a half. All I've done is spend time with a friend who tried to persuade me to buy a dress. Not exactly my thing to begin with."

Shit, fair point. "Yeah, right." *Smooth, real damn smooth, Monroe. Still, what would she look like in a dress?* When was the last time he'd seen her wear one? If she had worn a dress or a skirt he could have slid his hand up along the length of her thigh, teasing the soft skin before slipping his hand between her legs to cup the silken, inviting warmth he knew lay within easy reach.

Fuck.

Yup, that's exactly what he wanted to do. Repeatedly until neither of them could move.

"I'm sorry, but this isn't going to work," Corina turned and waved a server over, ordering a nonalcoholic drink before she turned back at him. The server hesitated a moment before he nodded once, his gaze meeting David's, only to return to his duties.

"What do you mean?" *What was that about?* He frowned and wanted to look at the server again. *No, focus on Corina.*

"One drink then I'm calling it a night. I've got much better things to do with my time." She glanced around the dining area before turning her attention back to him. "You have to agree is a waste of time."

Like hell, she was. "I don't think so. We agreed to this date, to get to know each other and that's what's going to happen. We're going to try to learn more about each other." *I can figure out your weaknesses and use them to rescue my brother, betray your trust, turn my best friend against me and ruin what's between us.*

Corina arched an elegant eyebrow. "And your idea of getting to know me better is sitting in silence? Wonderful move. Epic."

"Sorry. I'm not exactly used to this." David's jaw clenched. No, he didn't want to sit in silence, he wanted her stripped bare, bent over the table with his cock buried deep.

His balls tightened at the idea.

Last Name

Down boy.

But it was such a tempting image.

"Let's see, what don't you know about me? Hmm, let me think for a moment." She made a play of tapping one finger against her cheek. "I don't like being lied to or used. No, sorry, you know that one now, don't you?"

"Corina, please." *Begging won't help.* He had to think of a subject to talk about, one which was non-sexual and safe. "When did you last speak with either of your parents? You mentioned them once or twice when we were together."

Her shoulders stiffened, the color draining from her face. She took the drink from the server, drained it, a momentary frown creasing her brow before she set the glass down. "Why do you want to know?"

"I have to start somewhere." *Bad choice, obviously.* Still, he couldn't drop the subject now. Not without appearing weak. What was the issue about her parents anyway? Did it have to do with why she kept people at arm's length?

"Mom a year ago. Dad, closer to ten."

"Why leave it that long? You made it sound as if you were close – at least to your father. I assumed you – I mean – I thought you were still in contact with him when we were together." He'd have killed for one more chat with his dad, but it was never going to happen. Not unless he spoke through one of the Adepts of Thanatos. A waste of time as he didn't believe in the ability, to begin with, no matter how well docomeented their skills were. The dead stayed dead. They didn't come back to chat with you no matter how deeply he might want it to be otherwise.

But what was keeping Corina from talking to her parents? He couldn't let this go, if she didn't open up with him on this then she'd continue to hold back, to hide things from him and they'd be doomed before they'd begun.

"Does it matter?" She shrugged, the movement sharp and unfriendly.

"Obviously or you wouldn't be this upset about the question." Hadn't she spent time on Mars after they'd parted? He was missing something significant here and if he could get to the bottom of it then perhaps they'd have a chance after all.

Her entire body stiffened, her fingers laced in her lap, knuckles white as she pressed her lips into a tight, thin line.

"He's dead, what else matters." The two-word reply flat and emotionless. Small beads of sweat formed across her brow as she shifted in her seat.

No, not emotionless. Controlled. Her eyes glittered briefly before she blinked several times. Tears. Unshed tears.

"He's been dead for the full ten years? This isn't a recent thing?" What was she not telling him? Why hadn't she mentioned this detail three years ago? Who had she spent time with if not her father during her retraining on Mars? Or had she visited for another reason?

She nodded briskly.

"And your Mom is dead or alive?" *Please, don't let her have lost both of them. How could she have hidden all of this from me?* Had a part of Corina not trusted him back then? Not a pleasant concept.

"Alive." Again the clipped tone. Corina's right hand moved, barely a twitch, toward her comm before it stilled.

"She doesn't approve of your choice of career?" Okay, not dead, then what was going on between them? Career seemed the likely choice but...

"No."

Of course not. Why would she when she's a pleasure adept. "I see. I was told those of the adepts of Gaea were taught to accept all paths." What was he missing? What had upset her mother so much? Fuck, this was harder than he'd thought it would be.

No one had warned him this dating thing would be this hard. It wasn't as if he'd ever done this before, he'd always stumbled into encounters and Corina – what he'd had with Corina had been his first long term relationship.

"Yes."

I have to pull her out of these one-word answers. "What's her problem with your choice? Had she hoped you would follow her into the path of a pleasure adept? Or was it more?"

"My father."

Two words, it was an improvement if barely, however, she still wasn't looking at him. How the hell was he supposed to make sense of what was going on with her if all she'd give him were one- or two-word answers? "Woman, if you don't look at me, I'm going to have to walk over and hug you in front of everyone."

She flinched and forcibly turned to meet his gaze. Her eyes glittered no matter how many times she blinked to clear them, but still, she held his gaze. "Better?"

"Much, thank you," his arms ached with the need to hold her. "All right, she's upset with you because the path you've chosen might result in your death, as it did with your father. Is that it?"

"Yes."

Back to one-word answers. Wonderful. And she still wasn't telling him the entire truth. She'd spoke of her mother when they'd been together, if only in passing, and there hadn't been a cold, detached edge to the conversations. Fuck he couldn't do this. *I have to. I can't let her turn me aside by being cold. Maybe that's why she's this way? It's a part of her plan to keep me at arm's length?* "Who else have you told about this? You didn't mention it to me when we were first together."

"No one."

In ten years since her father's death, she'd not discussed this with anyone except her mother? How the hell had she managed to keep it all inside? The pain and grief locked up inside, with no outlet, no relief. Would he have been able to do it, go on alone with the weight on his shoulders? She was far stronger than he'd ever given her credit for, but was she also alone?

The idea didn't please him.

I should have been there to help her. Damnit, she could have turned to me, talk to me, cried with me. Why didn't she? Because she hadn't trusted him.

"Corina, why didn't you find a friend to discuss this with? One who could have helped you through the dark times? You can't spend the rest of your life at odds with your Mom. Not when it obviously hurts you…"

"Hurts me?" She glared, her gaze narrowing. "What the fuck would you care about me hurting after what you did? You can't expect me to buy that shit and how dare you judge me." Corina shook, violently, the glistening tears in her eyes spilling over down over flushed cheeks. "You don't know a thing about me except you like me in your bed." She pushed back the chair, staggering to her feet.

"Don't…" he moved to her side, wanting to hold her, protect her, shield her from the view of the few people who were now watching them. "You're not on your own now, love. Listen to me please; you don't have to shut everything behind walls for the rest of your life. If you'd let me…"

"Let you what? Walk out on me again? Tear me apart inside and spend a lifetime rebuilding because I trusted you when I knew better?" She shook her head but appeared unable or unwilling to move away from him. She glanced around and shuddered, struggling to control herself, but it wasn't working.

"Corina?" This wasn't like her at all. He leaned in, watching her closely.

"I-I don't know what's happening." She stammered, her eyes unfocused.

"Talk to me," he reached across the table, fingers brushing hers.

"Gods, I can't do this. This isn't me. I don't lose control like this. I can't let people see me like this." Her voice a whisper now. "Please, I don't know what's happening to me. David. I-I can't bring myself back under control."

Last Name

"Then let me help you, please. Let me walk you back to your quarters. Or at least get you…"

"Your ship."

She was shaking now, a soft tremble he noticed in her hands. "Are you sure?"

"Yes," a curt nod and the desperate glint in her eyes convinced him. "I'm sure."

Heading to his ship wasn't a wise idea, but as she leaned in close and let David lead the way through the station, her vision half-blinded by tears, she couldn't think of a better one. She wasn't herself no matter what else she wanted to believe, and going back to her quarters would be a mistake. His ship meant being able to truly close the door to the station.

They were close to the docking ring.

Gods, she couldn't think straight anymore, and it disconcerted her. What had happened? She wasn't like this, and it didn't make sense. Her body wasn't reacting the way it should. The way it had been trained to respond from a young age. She was losing control.

She'd never lost control in her life. Not even as a child – at least as far as she could recall. Her mother – *Mom, why did you turn your back on me?*

Fresh tears spilled down her cheeks. This wasn't how she was supposed to react.

Dad… why did you leave me? You weren't supposed to die this young. You were supposed to be the one man I could rely on.

She was exposed. Alone, she had to be alone, behind closed doors before she could let down the walls about her parents.

I want him back in my life. David. I want him back.

Hell no, she wasn't going down that road. And yet here she was, leaning on him emotionally and letting him help her.

She closed her eyes for a moment, trying to force her mind into order. A heavy, damp fog clouded her mind. This didn't make any sense. Add in the crying, the way she'd lost emotional control and she was at a loss on how to handle it.

She didn't break down like this. Crying was a weakness she didn't permit, not in public at least and she couldn't let it destroy her.

"Lean on me," he curled one arm about her waist, pulling her close. "I won't let you fall."

She shook her head, struggling to keep from collapsing. What had happened to her? She shouldn't be like this, not without reason. They'd been talking about her parents.

Gone, he left me. He walked into the fight, knowing he wasn't fit enough, knowing he was sick, and he did it anyway.

A hand wrapped tightly around her heart, squeezing it.

Can't breathe.

She stumbled only to find he kept her on her feet.

"Not far to go now."

She blinked and took in her surroundings. Had she lost track of time during the walk? *Think. You can get this under control.* Maybe she could, perhaps she couldn't. Right now she wasn't sure what day of the week it was.

What the hell had been in the drink anyway? He hadn't touched it, she'd made certain it never left her sight. Not that he was the type to drug her drink, no matter what she believed of him, he wasn't the type to pull such an underhanded stunt.

"I-I don't feel like myself." Her tongue and lips were numb. The drink hadn't been strong enough to do this to her, had it? No, it hadn't contained alcohol. She wouldn't drink if she had to go on duty. "Something's not right. I don't understand it, but it feels off."

"I'll get a medic to see you once we're on board." They'd stopped in front of the docking tube long enough for David to key in his access code, then they were no longer on the station proper but inside his ship.

"David…" She couldn't think, couldn't breathe without effort. "Please. I-I can't – can't breathe."

"Medic. Amber, get to medical, now."

His girlfriend? He hadn't mentioned a girlfriend. Why would he hide this woman? *I'll kill her, whoever she is.*

No, he wasn't the type to cheat. He's a decent man, at least she'd believed he was until he'd walked out on her. *How can it be cheating if we weren't together?*

"Captain?" A woman's voice filtered through the fog, claiming her mind. "What's going on?"

"She was fine, then cold, then emotional, now she can't stand up without help."

She wasn't walking anymore. When had that happened? It took several moments before Corina realized David was carrying her with her head nestled against his chest. She couldn't remember him picking her up.

"This the peacekeeper? The one you were planning on meeting? I wasn't aware you were bringing her back to the ship tonight, Captain."

"This is my wife." He picked up the pace.

"Wife? I don't understand. Married? When did that happen?" The woman choked on the words but kept up.

Oh, she doesn't like that detail. I don't like her either. She wasn't sure why she disliked the woman, but there was an air about her which set Corina's teeth on edge.

"Several years ago, I'll fill you in later."

What had changed? She was no longer warm, nor was she resting in his arms. Something firm supported her entire body and lights shone in her eyes. A bed? She groaned and closed her eyes, trying to shut out the brightness.

"Corina, can you hear me?" His voice broke through her musings though they barely made sense to her. At least not without effort.

"Hmm, yes. Head hurts." She groaned again and tried to roll on her side. Her stomach lurched, but she refused to vomit. *Fuck, this isn't happening.* Had she picked up a bug from one of the many races who visited the station? No, it had come on too fast for any illness she knew about.

"She's been drugged, that much is obvious but with what is the real question," a new voice. Male this time. "Step back please, Captain. I'll need to get the readings before I can treat her."

Drugged? Okay, it made sense. She wasn't losing her mind then or having a nervous breakdown. Oddly enough, the knowledge calmed her. She didn't react this way normally, maybe the drug was to blame whatever it was. *Of course, it's a drug, I'd have figured it out if I wasn't feeling this damned out of it.*

A beeping caught her attention. A com? Hers? No, the sound was wrong. Damnit, she couldn't think straight. *This can stop now. Like right now.*

"Message coming in. Amber, Shiel, I have to step out for a moment," David's voice. Leaving? What was so important he had to vanish now? He was supposed to be here, helping her, not walking out and leaving her in the hands of a stranger.

He's a ship's captain. He has other things to deal with.

But she was ill, drugged. He should agree to stay with her. Take care of her. If she wanted another else to tend her, she would have said Piotr or the med techs on the station. Not here. Not his ship.

I don't need looking after.

Oh hell yeah, she did. A part of her knew and accepted it.

"Understood, Captain. She's in good hands. Amber will stay with me in case I need assistance."

"I will?" The woman inquired; her voice sharp. "All right, fine. Not like I have better things to do with my time."

Bitch. You and I are going to have words when I'm feeling more like myself. Long, painful words.

"Step back, I need clear readings here." The medic instructed. Shiel? Had that been his name? She couldn't begin to guess which planet the name initially came from. Gods, she could barely think, let alone think straight.

Her head throbbed, and she swallowed, trying to keep the

contents of her stomach where they belonged. When had she last been this ill?

Never. I don't get ill. Injured yes. Ill no.

"Toxins are taking a bit to identify. Not naturally occurring, a modification of an illness from the Travis system. Interesting..." The medic's voice trailed off.

Interesting in a fun way, or a bad? What was it with doctors and their use of the word interesting? *Hello, the sick person on the table would like to know what's going on. Speak up, please.*

"Modified means this was a deliberate attempt?" Amber was closer to the table by the sound of her voice than Shiel appeared to be. What was she doing here, anyway? Hadn't Amber been about to leave? The woman didn't belong here.

"Yes, this type of thing doesn't happen by accident unless you work in a lab or a badly run storage facility," Shiel explained in a cool, calm tone.

"Poisoning," Amber's voice trailed off.

Poisoned. How? Who would want to try and drug her? Why would they do it to her? She was a Peacekeeper.

Revenge?

One of the people she'd arrested?

Gods, she still couldn't think straight, and it was about to drive her crazy. Not the interesting kind of crazy either. The homicidal kill them all crazy, and the first one on her to kill list was this Amber chick.

"Drugged, not poisoned. It won't kill her, but she'll feel like shit for a while. Once we get things moving smoothly, she'll be back on her feet in a matter of hours." Shiel continued to explain.

"Wh-what is it? What's in my system?" Corina forced the words out. She didn't dare open her eyes, not with how her head was now swimming, but hopefully, it would pass. "And c-can you do anything about how I feel?"

A hand touched the side of her face, calm, precise, and professional. "You've been dosed with a chemically adapted strain of what's been called Travian Flu. Likely through food or drink as it needs a sugar-heavy host to survive prior to ingestion and you'd have noticed an injection. You're confused and out of control emotionally is understandable with what's been used."

Travian Flu, she wasn't a medic, but it didn't sound like fun. Food or drink? She'd had a drink with David, could that have been it? If so, why wasn't he ill? She didn't like where this was going. She was the target.

Enemy. Personal. Another woman, maybe? Many professionals believe women preferred drugs and poison, although Corina knew there were enough out there who enjoyed getting physical. Especially if they had Mars or Valhallian blood in their background.

"Need this dealt with." She debated opening her eyes a crack but rejected the idea with the next wave of nausea. "Don't like this."

"Working on it, but the only thing I have will make you feel a little drunk."

Drunk had to be better than how she felt right now, didn't it? "Do it," she murmured, her hands pressed against her stomach. "Please."

"It will take a few minutes to synthesize, try to relax," Shiel explained, and patted her lightly on the shoulder and moved away from the bed.

A few minutes. She could wait that long, couldn't she?

Like I have a choice.

"You did what?" David snapped at the holographic figure. This wasn't happening. This fucking shit wasn't happening to them. What the hell had Blain been thinking of when he'd decided on this course of action? "Tell me again, using small words, I get what you're saying here."

"I arranged for Lieutenant Greenheart to be drugged, therefore making it easier to reclaim Drake," the middle-aged man explained calmly. "It appeared likely you'd escort her to sickbay, and once she was in their care, it would only be natural to check in on her. Such an occurrence should make it easier to lift the security codes you would need or relieve her of her pass. Either would work in making the successful retrieval of our agent possible. I presume you took advantage of the situation once the drug hit her system."

"No sir, I didn't." *Fuck. Does he have any understanding of what he's done?* David stared at Commander Blain and tried to force his mind into a semblance of order. "Sir, I don't think it was the wisest course of action. Corina Greenheart isn't going to take this well when she finds out what happened to her, and she will figure out who was behind it sooner or later. She's an intelligent woman, and the men and women she works with didn't lack in intelligence either. Kraven, for instance, has to be one of the best I've had the privilege to work with outside of the Rangers." Shit, if the man didn't have a damn good career ahead of him with the Peacekeepers, he'd have suggested recruiting Kraven years ago.

"It worked, didn't it? The peacekeeper is unwell and in medical." Blain shrugged, his tone cold. "I don't see the problem here. You should be able to collect her codes or pass without a problem. Once you've duplicated them, she will be none the wiser until it's too late."

"She's onboard." *Deal with it asshole.*

Blain's mouth dropped open for a moment then closed. "What the hell made you bring her onboard?"

"I believed it was for the best." Okay, not entirely true. It had been Corina's idea, but Blain didn't need to know.

"It wasn't in the plan."

"You mean the plan you failed to tell me about? Screw the fucking plan. She's an old friend... my wife actually... and we were-"

"She's your what? Did I hear you correctly?" Blain spluttered and leaned over, picking up a datapad. "Married? I don't remember anything of that nature on your record. No, your record is clean. When did this happen? Why didn't you report this detail? It's a breach of protocol."

Shit, this wasn't the way he'd wanted it on record. "We married when we met the last time, I didn't see a need to add to my report as it was a part of the cover."

Blain's frown deepened, his gaze narrowing. "The relationship was a part of the cover, but you weren't ordered to marry her. Of all the stupid, bloody things to do."

"It doesn't matter. We are officially, and in the eyes of Gaea and Mars, man and wife." *In the eyes of Gaea and Mars, we're man and wife as far as I'm concerned. Anything else is icing on the cake.*

"Gods." Blain shook his head and turned away before he set the pad down again. "Shit, this — you should have told me. This could blow up more than — no, no, I'll figure it out."

"You've put me in a position where I'm not only meant to betray a longtime friendship but where I'm forced to consider betraying my wife for the second time since we married." Which one mattered to him the most? It wouldn't have been long ago he'd have said Kraven, but now...

Corina. I don't want to hurt her again. Shit, I never wanted to hurt her the first time. He hadn't thought the entire situation through. A lame excuse, but then he'd simply enjoyed and obeyed.

"Perhaps there's another way then. You said in the eyes of Mars?" Blain rubbed his chin thoughtfully. "That's her background, isn't it? Mars and Gaea?"

"Yes, sir." What was the man up to this time? If he had plans to harm Corina any further, then all hell was about to break loose. At this point, he didn't trust Blain, not after what the man had pulled. What if the dosing had been wrong and she'd died? Had Blain worked through the possible ramifications of such a mistake?

Would he care?

No, of course, he wouldn't. Corina was nothing to him. A

member of the peacekeepers, yes, but expendable as she wasn't an agent of the Shadow Rangers and Blain wouldn't hesitate to dispose of Corina if it suited his plans.

"A challenge match would be one way, but she'll be recovering from the drug. A formal bride kidnapping…"

"Sir, I don't understand how you think it might work in regards to rescuing Drake." How the hell was he supposed to kidnap his wife and free his brother? This was fucking ridiculous. The man was insane. Worse, Blain was expecting him to pull off the impossible.

"Best if you don't know at this time, Monroe. I'll be in contact. Blain out." The holographic image flickered and vanished.

Decoy, he wants me to act like a fucking decoy while he sends another in to get my brother. Shit. This wasn't going to work. How did Blain think Corina would react to being kidnapped? She'd explode, but no, it was his problem, not Blain's, at least as far as his commanding officer was concerned.

Fuck. He's screwed me this time.

David rubbed his temples and paced around the room. This was a bad idea. Worst idea he'd ever been presented with. Oh, sure, it might actually work as a decoy long enough to yank Drake out of the shit storm he was obviously in, but then what? Corina would kill him and Kraven…

Kraven would be pissed but wouldn't assume the kidnapping was anything more, and the timing with Drake would simply be bad timing.

This might work.

Chapter Eight

David turned off the screen and leaned back in his chair. Had he remembered his research about Mars correctly? If he had, it could work. The harebrained scheme of Blain's might actually tip things in his favor, but only if she still followed the old codes. He'd have to ask her, of course, but how to do it without tipping her off?

The drug? Would work?

If she wanted revenge, she could go about it in several different ways, including following full legal actions as would be best suited to a peacekeeper. However, if she followed the old codes, then he could use them against her, and gain her as his wife once and for all, as well as providing the correct level of distraction for Drake's rescue. If he could probe, find out where she stood on such things, then he'd have enough information to work from.

There was a chance it could work. A slim one but it might be worth the risk. Not that Blain was giving him much of a choice here. Damn man was pushing on the one thing which might put Corina in his arms for the rest of their lives, but would she be able to live with the outcome?

Would he?

Yes. Maybe. Shit, I don't know.

If he remembered the details correctly, a warrior had the right to kidnap then challenge for mating rights. It was a tradition which still existed on Mars, just as the right of the hunt did. Though outside of Mars, Valhalla and their colonies, he hadn't heard of either being used and he might have a few problems convincing Kraven he'd done the right thing. At least until Corina informed the man, this was within the traditions of her people, and the prior claim David had made such a justifiable action beyond the boundaries of Mars.

Last Name

And she might fight. Especially if I get one part of the challenge or kidnapping rites wrong.

Then there was the drug issue, if she were still processing it through her system, she'd be too weak to be able to fight back, which would make both forms of claiming out of the question. It was seen as a form of cowardice to use a weakness to gain the advantage when claiming a mate. One thing he could agree with as far as the traditions were concerned.

He'd have to give her the chance to recover before he tried to capture her. It was pointless, but traditions weren't to be argued with. Using a weakness created by another enemy was frowned upon at the best of times by her people, and it sat ill with him now he had the chance to think about it. If he was going to do this, he had to do it the right way.

I'm not going to let her slip through my fingers. Not this time. Even if it means following an outdated set of rituals.

His cock throbbed at the idea of both types of challenges. Hunting Corina down, binding her and bringing her back to his tent, or whatever, as a captured prize, had its appeal. But beating her in a fair fight before claiming her was more his style. Their arguments had always had the knock-on effect of leaving them both at least partially aroused. Maybe there was a way they could combine the two? He couldn't chase Corina through the station, bind her and haul her off over his shoulder without being stopped.

He bit back a groan and rearranged himself. Images of torn clothing, sweat coated skin and Corina moving beneath him, pleading, arching, wanting more, needing...

"Captain?" Amber's voice roused him from his musings.

"Yes?" He turned in the chair and smiled.

"Your guest is awake, according to Shiel." Amber's voice hardened on the word guest. "I believe you wanted to be informed when such occurred, Captain."

"Amber, sit down a moment," he gestured to the spare seat in his room. If there was a problem, he had to get to the bottom of it now before the situation got out of hand. When had the problem started? Thinking back it had to be from the moment he'd told Amber Corina was his wife.

Wonderful, exactly what I need to complicate the situation. As if he needed any more problems right now.

Amber frowned but then did as she was told. "Is there a problem, Captain?"

"I'm not sure, which is I why I want to discuss this with you." He sealed the door, invoking the privacy shield before he continued. "You have an issue with Lieutenant Greenheart. Or am I picking up on signals which simply don't exist?"

Amber stiffened instantly.

"I'd like to know what the problem is before we take any steps to resolve it." The way the woman reacted said it all.

"No problem, Captain. Now, if that's all…" she moved to her feet and took a step toward the closed door.

"Sit down."

Her jaw tightened, but she obeyed. "Captain, this is a waste of time. We both have other matters to attend to."

"I believe otherwise. And it's obvious there is an issue, or you wouldn't react this way. Amber, I've known you for two years now and you stiffen anytime she's mentioned, glare at her, or act as if you're made of ice. What the hell is going on here?" *Why doesn't she like my wife? Have they met before, and there's been a problem between them?*

Amber's hands clenched into fists.

"Amber?"

"She's the one, isn't she?" Her voice was clipped.

"Sorry?" Was he missing a piece of the puzzle? "The one what?"

"The reason you won't look at me or any other woman. The reason you don't take lovers, or one-night stands." The words were choked, forced through clenched teeth. "She's the one who ruined you for any other woman."

"Ruined me?" He frowned and met Amber's gaze, he wouldn't have put it that way. No, never ruined. "Is she the one I love, yes, but why does it matter to you?"

"Gods, you're blind. I've been trying since the day I grabbed the berth on this ship, to get you to notice me. All I've ever wanted when I've been around you is to have you see me as a woman. Not only as a member of your crew." She pushed back to her feet, shoulders taut, hands clenched, eyes blazing with fury. "You've never looked at me as if I'm a woman. I'm nothing more than another member of the crew, an interchangeable part of the machinery. One piece much the same as the next." Tears glimmered in her eyes, and she blinked, trying to control them. "And it's her fault. A woman I never knew existed until today."

"I work with you..." Corina's fault he'd never fallen in love with Amber? No, he didn't see it that way but apparently Amber did.

"And it doesn't stop others from being involved in shipboard romances." She snapped at him. "I've tried everything short of crawling naked into your bunk. What did I have to do to get you to look at me? To see me the way a man is supposed to see a woman?"

How was he supposed to handle this? "Amber, she's my wife. It's not just a story I've told others to get them to back off. Corina and I are married. She's asked for a divorce, but I'm not ready to turn my back on her." He'd never been ready for, he'd had to leave, he'd had no choice. "She's mine, and I'm not going to walk away from her again. I made that mistake once before but I can't – I won't make it again." Now he knew he couldn't leave the woman who had remained in his heart in the three years they'd been apart.

"I understand, Captain and I'll put the word out I'm searching for another berth as soon as possible." Amber blinked and tried to smile. A smile which didn't quite reach her eyes.

"Amber, you don't have to do this." What was the woman thinking? He had no problem working with her.

"Yes, Captain, I do. Eventually, I'd come to truly hate you for not looking at me the way you do her. I'd rather leave on a good note than be removed on a bad. I'm sure you can understand. At least I hope you can."

Of all the things he'd expect, this was not one of them. "Is this the only workable option for you, Amber?" She was a damned fine member of his crew and losing her was not an idea which sat well with him but what other choice did he have?

"Unless you're about to tell me it's all in my mind. That the woman you've brought to this ship means little or nothing to you and I have a chance?" She met his gaze, but there was no hope in her eyes. "No, of course not. I'm no fool, and I know this woman, this wife of yours, means far more than you're able to voice right now. Let's not speak of hopes I know do not exist and instead part on a level footing, Captain."

Protesting wouldn't change a damned thing. Not for either of them, and the truth of the matter was he was spoken for. Amber was a damned fine woman and, if this was how she felt, she deserved the truth. Though it would lose him an officer, he had come to rely upon.

He said the only thing he could and remain the type of Captain he wanted to be. "I understand, Amber. I might not like your decision, but I'll respect it."

Corina blinked against the sharp lights and groaned. Someone had taken up residence behind her eyes and was merrily tunneling through her skull with picks and axes. The drunken stage had passed several hours ago, and she'd been left with the wonderful aftereffects of it all without the pleasure of enjoying the drink which had led to this.

Not like I drink much, to begin with.

Taking enough time off work to enjoy a drink with a friend was a rarity, and after this, she wasn't planning on trying out the heavy drinking thing anytime soon.

Bloody nightmare, the entire thing.

At first, she'd had visions of David taking advantage of her, dragging her off to his quarters and shutting out the universe, but it hadn't happened. No sex, only brief visits with minimal physical contact, then he'd leave again. Oh, he'd make sure Shiel was looking after her, and her health was improving, she was out of danger. Not as much as a kiss to help her through the torment.

Damn the man, at least he could have given me an excuse for wanting to fuck him.

"You're appear to be on the mend, Lieutenant Greenheart." Shiel walked over to the bed with a scanner in hand. "Your body is clear of the drug, and you're recovering. I need to get more fluids into you to be on the safe side. Once you're back to normal, then we can discuss releasing you from my care. A detail I'm sure you'll be glad to hear. "

"And do you have anything for my head?" She gave a wry smile. Fluids sounded ideal. Her mouth gummy, and her throat scratchy. "I've got a marching band in here, and they're hitting the wrong keys. I think they're doing it on purpose to see how long it will take before I kill one of them."

"Not yet, we need to get you hydrated first. I'll get you a glass of water, once you can show me you can hold it down, we'll move onto medication for the pain." He glanced up from the scanner and flashed what might have been an attempt at a smile. It never reached his eyes.

Medics. Sadists the lot of them. Piotr would get on with this one. War stories, they'd exchange war stories. Oh, and new methods to torture patients.

"I'm okay to sit up?" Like she would try drinking laying down, but she'd been told to do stranger things by medics.

"Yes, but you need to take it slow and easy. If you feel dizzy or nauseous, then stop and let me know." He offered one hand to steady her while the head of the bed moved, assisting her into a sitting position.

Corina struggled against the urge to close her eyes again and tried to focus on what she was seeing instead of what her mind told her was happening. What was it with medics? The cure was often worse than the illness.

Okay, not precisely true this time, but damn it all, my head's killing me.

"Better?"

"Yes, thank you."

Shiel gave a brief smile and, with scanner in hand, he wandered back through the small medical section, muttering under his breath.

"You appear normal again," David said from just inside the door.

"Shiel appears pleased with my progress." At least Amber wasn't with him. There was an air about the woman which made her skin itch. But David, at least he'd returned to check on her. Pity he hadn't been able to sit her in a private room where they could have become more intimate.

Her stomach protested the idea, quickly joined by the off-key members of her own personal band. Okay, maybe she needed to wait a little longer before she curled up with him. Like a lot longer, until her body was on her side once more.

"I was worried about you for a while." He hadn't moved from the door. Odd, what did he want? It was more than to check in on her. "I'm glad Shiel was able to help you with all of this."

"Yeah, thanks for that, I'm not sure where the poison came from, but I'll find out. I need to get back to the station soon. I'll have to report into Kraven unless you let him know what was going on?" Kraven would have a foaming fit. One of his officers poisoned? Though she'd been off duty at the time, he'd still take it personally. Okay, drugged was closer to the mark than poison but he'd still be upset about it. Such acts weren't honorable and, like Corina, he took matters of honor seriously.

"No, I didn't mention it to him. I believed it best if you and Shiel handled it. You know how medics are."

"Good," she'd deal with it when she was back on the station and able to lay the situation out to Kraven fully, along with her declaration she'd hunt the bastard who'd drugged her down and skin him, for shits and giggles.

David frowned before he sat down on the edge of the bed. "You're going after the guy responsible for this, aren't you?"

"Yes," like there was any other choice? A coward had taken her down, and she didn't know why. For all, she knew she hadn't been the real target. Hell, her being the target didn't make sense, to begin with.

"I see, and if it eats into the time we have left together, it's no problem for you, is it?"

Her heart dropped into the pit of her stomach. "It's not like that. It's a matter of honor."

"A Mars warrior thing, right?"

"Yeah." It was also a hunt the bastard down and get even thing, but it would have sounded petty. No, better he believed it was tied in with the codes of her father's people. *My people, not his. Mine.* "You understand, don't you?"

"No, I can't say I understand, not fully, but I'm not going to be able to persuade you otherwise, am I?" He sighed and rested one hand on her arm. "I know this is a part of your nature, your background, but I don't like it."

How could she explain it to him without sounding like a revenge-seeking maniac? What did it matter if she appeared insane anyway? She wasn't going to let this bastard get away with it, whoever he was. "The Adepts of Gaea have their own codes of honor, but it's those of Mars, of the warrior caste, that I was always drawn to. I was taught both but allowed to choose which path better suited me." Though her mother regretted giving her the choice in the first place. Oh, she'd have a field day with this situation. No doubt there would be endless lectures over why entering the peacekeepers had been the wrong choice. There would be theories her mother would force down her throat in an attempt to get Corina to turn from Mars to the loving arms of mother Gaea. "You either accept this is simply who I am, or you sign the papers and let me go. No half measures on this, no leeway. I'm not going to turn my back on the codes. They're all I'll have left at the end of the day."

Say you'll stay. Say you want me and will be here with me. Say you'll help me hunt the bastard down. No, she couldn't tell him, she'd never live it down. He'd have a power over her she'd never be able to take back.

"Are you sure those codes are all you'd have left?" He shook his head and continued. "No, I'm not looking for a fight with you, please believe me. One night, love. I'm asking for one night with me on board my ship, with no distractions. I'm owed that much I believe. Go and talk to Kraven then come back to me." He lifted his hand from her arm and cupped her cheek. "Is it too much to ask for after everything we meant to each other?"

Yes. No. Oh, Gods... I don't know anymore.

She tensed and fought against the urge to lean into his caress. It would have been damned easy to forget the universe and sink into the warm he offered. Safety, love, protection, all the things her Gaean side craved. Strength, aggression, the desire to fight and tumble her to the floor were exactly what her Mars side needed. He could please both halves of her nature. Why should she tell him no?

Why should she shut off a large part of who she was when he was offering her a chance to tear down the walls, if only for a time? Tear them down and find out precisely what she'd been hiding for all of these years.

"I don't know," she sighed and pulled away, reluctantly, from his hand. "I need to talk to Kraven first, figure a few things out and then-"

"Then you'll come back to me for one night." Not a question, a statement.

No, tell him no. This would be a mistake. He'll change me. He'll try and change me, and I'm too weak right now. Too damn weak and he knows it.

She licked, nervously, across her lips. He wasn't asking for the universe. A night. A single night. Not such a big deal if she wanted to be honest about it.

"We owe each other one night. I'm asking you to think about it, Corina. Think before you make a decision."

Perhaps he was right.

"All right, one night. I can't and won't promise more, but I'll give you the one night."

"Drugged? Are you positive?" Kraven stood up slowly from behind his desk, his face pale and drawn. "Shit, that's all we need. We've got a prisoner exchange taking place tomorrow afternoon, and I'm going to need you in top form. Are you certain they cleared it from your system? This isn't something we can run a risk with, not with so much going on."

"Yes, sir," she offered him the data chip. She couldn't provide much, but at least Shiel had been willing to provide the data both Piotr, and Kraven would need. "There's a full explanation of what happened here, and how it was treated, also I'm now fit for duty. The same information has been passed onto Piotr." And there was a man who had been extremely unhappy with the news. Those from Valhalla took a dim view on drugs and poisoning as did those from Mars. It was a coward's weapon, and those who used such tools weren't to be trusted.

Which, oddly enough, matched her own personal belief about the one who had attacked her.

"I'll have to confirm it with Piotr." He took the chip and set it in the reader. "If he clears you then I'll accept it. If he doesn't, I don't want to hear any arguments from you. I'll also be insisting on a full check-up."

"Understood, sir." Oh, she understood the issues. If there was a trace of the drug in her system, then it might impede her ability to work. Better to err on the side of caution and the report of a man Kraven trusted than the report from a stranger.

"If he clears you, then you'll be back on duty tomorrow in time for the transfer. I'll need my best people for this one, and that includes you. We'll have six other officers involved, including myself. Details are on a need to know and the rest of the details you don't need to know until ten hundred hours. Clear?" He glanced at the reader, frowning.

"Clear, sir." She had nothing to fear, and she needed to be back at work if for no other reason than to help her stay sane once David left the station.

"Now, do I need to ask what you were doing on Captain Monroe's ship?" Kraven glanced away from the reader. "Or should I leave it to my all too overactive imagination?"

She could tell him it was a personal matter, but she owed Kraven the truth. She took a deep breath, steadied her nerves, and explained. "Sir, David and I were – are – married. It was a mistake which happened several years ago, and we're trying to come to terms with and decide how best to rectify matters." She met his gaze, refusing to turn away. She had nothing to be ashamed of and nothing to fear. Did it matter if she'd agreed to one more night with him? It would give them a chance to mend fences and part on better terms.

Or change his mind and get him to stay at the station.

It wasn't going to happen.

"Ah, I see," Kraven nodded slightly. He closed his eyes for a moment before he continued, his voice oddly calm as he took care to meet her gaze again as he spoke. "The marriage mentioned in your files, though you were careful not to add it was still current, or who the marriage bound you to. Interesting you decided to leave that information out of the files at the time. I did wonder at the time, but you have the right, under peacekeeper codes, to keep the details to yourself as long as you were able to swear it wouldn't affect your work or loyalty oath. Obviously, it's not been a problem for you. Still…now I am curious as to what, exactly, is going on."

Okay, she'd known that would be coming. She coughed, trying to gain a moment to phrase things correctly. "It's because I didn't know his real name, sir. Not when I filled those forms in. I found out a few days after he left, he'd married me while undercover. It wasn't until a couple of months ago I found out, through channels, that his real name might be Monroe. By then, I saw no reason to add the information to my files." She finally turned her attention to him again, her cheeks heat streaked. "There were other reasons, of course. Ones I didn't want to go into."

"You were embarrassed by the situation." Kraven pressed obviously unwilling to let the matter rest. "Understandable but awkward."

Corina nodded, grateful he wasn't pressing for more information than she was ready to supply. "Yes, sir."

"It's not my business to ask, but I will anyway. Do you plan on seeing him again before his ship is due to depart?" Nothing mocking in his tone, or teasing in the way he watched her. Only concern.

He thinks of me as a friend. Damnit, I didn't expect that. The shock hit her square in the gut, but she buried it as best she could. "Yes, tonight in fact. A last meeting. I'm hoping he will then sign the papers, but I doubt it. He's stubborn about the situation." He'd stall, change his mind, or change hers. Gods, did she actually want him to no longer be a part of her life? Never to feel his touch again?

No.

Her stomach knotted in rebellion. She couldn't let this happen. Losing him, seeing him walk out of her life again, was more than she could take. What other choice did she have? They were walking different paths in life. He had his ship, and she had her career with the peacekeepers, and neither of them was willing to give up on their chosen careers.

"This will be a farewell meeting between you two?" Kraven's voice softened as he observed her. "I understand. Watch your heart, Corina. You're a decent woman, a strong woman, one who needs an equal in your life. If he's not the one you are meant to be with then you will heal, eventually and you won't be alone. I'll be here, and you have other friends on the station who will willingly help you through it. Do not try and go through this on your own if you and Monroe decide to part."

"Is that an order, sir?" Of all the things Corina had expected Kraven to say, it hadn't been this. If it were an order then, of course, she'd do her best to follow it, but she'd resent it. Gods, how she'd resent it. He had no right to…

"No."

"Then thank you," she smiled, nervously, shifting her weight from one foot to the other. Time was ticking away on her, stealing minutes she could spend with David. Moments they might never have again, and she didn't want to lose a single one of them. "May I have permission to depart?"

"I'll see you tomorrow, Lieutenant Greenheart."

Chapter Nine

David rubbed his temples, his stomach in knots. Fuck. What was he thinking of here? There were many things which could go wrong and yet he knew he'd go through with this. After the long talk he'd had with Blain, the snatch and grab was the only chance he had to get his brother out of danger, and still potentially have a relationship with Corina. It meant adapting the kidnapping rite, but it was still within the boundaries of what was acceptable. If the challenge worked then...

Then what?

He'd have to tell her the truth about his work before they entered into the challenge. The only fair thing to do and he could go over it tonight before anything else happened between them. As for the challenge -- sure, she had the blood of a warrior running through her veins, but would it work? She could still fight the relationship, push him away, but she couldn't deny the bond between them. Not unless she wanted to turn her back on her father's traditions.

Which she won't.

Amber was another matter. Fuck, he hadn't expected a complication. Despite their talk and his request she rethink her decision, she'd already put in for a transfer to another vessel, and if things worked out, she'd be moving to a new ship before he left with Corina.

How the hell had he missed that one? Had loving Corina left him blind?

Amber was a stunning woman, with a level of confidence which had hidden, from David, the way she'd looked at him. But the signs had all been present. Her attention, the way she'd watched him, the care in making sure the smallest task was completed beyond his expectations. She'd been in love with him from the first day she'd stepped onto the ship. Oh, he could see and kicked himself for it. If he'd been willing to see the problem, then maybe Amber would still be a part of the crew and meeting up with Corina again wouldn't have opened the door to new issues.

Nothing he could do about it now except recommend her to any Captain interested in hiring her on. She deserved nothing less, and it was the only thanks he could give her for the service she had given to the ship.

No, she deserved to be happy, with a man who loved her or who could love her. Instead, he could only help transfer her to a new ship and hope for the best. *Then why do I feel so shitty about all of this? It's not like I hurt her on purpose.* No, he hadn't but it didn't change things, and he now felt like the worst heel possible.

Amber isn't my responsibility.

Not true – she was until he found her another ship Amber remained a member of his crew, his responsibility and though she'd be gone shortly he wasn't about to forget. *I should have seen what was going on, but there's nothing I can do to change things now. Not sure there was anything I could have done if I had realized it before running into Corina again.*

No point in beating himself up about this.

Corina.

He glanced at the time.

Another ten minutes and she'd be here, but he needed to double check a few things first. Everything had to be right to the smallest detail. He had one shot at this. One and no more. He had to get it right. No second chances, do-overs and it was likely she'd kill him if she found out the secondary reason for the snatch and grab.

The room was prepared for their night together and come the morning – then he'd follow tradition and see if it led him to heaven or hell, or perhaps somewhere in between. As for tonight, this was their time before he opened up Pandora's Box and let loose the troubles of mankind. Or at least the wrath of an angry female warrior with murder on her mind.

She won't go that far.

Only time would tell. She'd have reason to kill him if she did find out what he was doing. Fuck, this was insane, but it was the only option he had if he wanted to keep Corina in his life.

"Captain, Amber is requesting a few moments before she departs the ship for the last time." His com officer announced through the open link. "Are you available?"

Was he? A part of him wanted to avoid the farewell, but Amber had served him and the ship well in the time she had been a part of his crew. If he was going to go through with this better to get it done in public with plenty of witnesses around. "Yeah, I'll be there in two. I need to finish work here." *And a couple of minutes to compose myself before I face off with a woman who was – is in love with me.*

"Understood, Captain." The line closed.

Did the others know how Amber had wanted him? If they did, they'd kept it to themselves, and he doubted they'd say anything to him.

"Captain," Amber nodded once as he walked onto the bridge. "Thank you for coming, it's appreciated."

What was he supposed to say? She'd been in his life long enough he knew Amber would be missed, not only by himself but for the others who had worked with her. "I'm sorry to see you go, Amber. I wish things could have been different. You've been a vital part of this crew." He should say more, so much more, but what good would it do either of them?

She nodded again and glanced around the bridge. "I had hoped I'd found my last berth here."

"I understand." He watched Amber, trying to figure out what he needed to say. "You could change your mind and stay with us. No problem if that's what you wanted to do."

The smile that touched her lips was a sorrowful one. "No, we both know it isn't possible, Captain. Besides, I've already received three offers of berths, and one of them would mean heading into the central systems. I'm waiting on information from core control."

Depending on what Blain wanted, Amber might find herself taking a berth on a civilian vessel. Such was risky, but also not unheard of, and she had enough experience to be sent on such a mission. A woman like Amber would be an excellent addition to any crew. She'd be able to find her place and get on with her work, dealing with any mission Blain and the Rangers threw at her.

Sooner or later she'd be the captain of her own ship.

Three ships, though? He shouldn't have been surprised, she was talented, and the review he'd provided for her would have been enough to get her a berth on any ship out there. "And you've got yourself a temp room on the station?" He had to know, especially with what was about to happen.

"For one night, yes. I'll be in my new berth come the morning either way. You know how core command works. They don't let us sit around on our asses, waiting for the perfect sunrise."

Odd, in space or on stations, they still used morning, afternoon and evening, but it was a routine he'd grown used to. "Understood."

For a moment, silence enfolded those on the deck, and David became all too aware of the way the others were watching them. Watching him.

"Permission to leave, Captain?" Amber's calm voice drew his attention. "Unless there's anything else we need to discuss."

"You have my permission and blessing, Amber. Thank you, again, for everything you've done both for the ship and myself." He held out his right hand, hoping she would take it.

A man coughed behind him, but he didn't turn to see who it was.

A console beeped, but he kept his focus on Amber, waiting to see what she would do. She deserved that much from him at least. *I can't give her anything else, but I can give her the respect she deserves.*

Last Name

She slipped her small, steady hand into his and shook, a slight smile gracing her lips. "Thank you, Captain. For welcoming me, and for accepting why I need to leave. If things didn't work between us, I can be thankful for the chance I had in serving with you."

He glanced down at their linked hands and, for a moment only, wondered what it might have been like between him. Then it was gone. There was only one woman for him, and she would be in his arms soon enough. A woman he'd have to fight to win. Fight in more ways than he'd ever expected, but she was worth it.

He stood and watched as Amber left the ship, pushing his concerns and doubts to the back of his mind. She'd be fine. There was a place for her, and a man for her, somewhere in the future, and he was doing the right thing by letting her go instead of offering her false hope.

Yes, it's the right damn thing to do.

"I'll be spending time with Corina when she arrives." He turned to take in the men and women of his crew, or at least those who remained. "But what hasn't been officially said is Corina Greenheart is my wife." He glanced around, but no one appeared to be shocked. Okay, Amber or Shiel had let the information slip.

He lifted his head, straightened his shoulders, and did his best to make sure there wasn't a trace of doubt in his features.

"Corina and I still have a few things to work out, and she will be told what I do – as it's a part of the reason why we didn't work out the first time. We don't know what we're going to do, but once a decision has been made, I will inform you all. You'll have a right to know, and I'm not about to keep secrets of this nature from you all. Too many of those of late and we work with enough secrets as it is." He owed them that much, this business with Amber had shown him the dangers of keeping things buried.

No more.

He had to change, not only for Corina but for himself. It was time to grow the fuck up.

"Should we be wishing you luck?" Shiel's sardonic smile broke lit his features. "Or helping you with an escape plan?"

"I haven't made up my mind about that yet," David admitted.

A nervous laugh rippled through his crew.

"Fair. Shit, I don't know what I'd do if I was suddenly faced with a woman I was apparently married to and telling her what you do, what we all do, it means you trust this woman, and we've got to support you." Shiel admitted and took a step closer. "If we can help, we will. Amber's gone, and we knew, we all knew how she felt. All of us except you apparently."

Ouch.

"How long?"

"Within two days of her joining the crew." The Navigator admitted from her post. "It was kinda obvious, at least to me, the way she watched you. Oh, she was careful about it, but she couldn't hide it all the time."

"Took me about three weeks," Shiel added with a slight shrug. "But hey, I'm a guy – it takes us a bit longer to put the pieces into place."

Double ouch.

"You're planning on winning her over?" His Navigator grinned. "Cool, we're here if you need us to lock her in a room until she sees sense or another insane plan. Whatever works, right?"

"Yeah, whatever works."

One night. That's all she'd agree to, one night in his arms as friends and lovers before they parted company. Maybe he'd sign the papers and perhaps he wouldn't, but she wasn't going to worry about it right now. Maybe he'd tell her, finally, what was going on with him? Either way, for once she was going to relax and enjoy the moment.

Yeah right.

Okay, she was going to try and relax so she could enjoy it.

Last Name

He was skilled in bed, and she'd never regretted the time they'd spent together in bed. It was the rest of the mess, which was the problem. All of the dangers getting involved would bring such as him tearing her heart in two when he left.

And he would leave.

No, she wasn't going to think about it she was, however, going to think about all of the dirty, outrageous things they'd done together. The way their bodies slapped together. Sweat dripping off their flesh. Their bodies one as they groaned and enjoyed each other.

Oh yeah, much better.

She smoothed her hands over her hair before she took the final steps down the corridor toward the connection tube which would lead into his ship, but instinct stopped her in her tracks. If he didn't like how she appeared then she'd turn around, walk away and be done with it. But she knew this wasn't about how she looked. It was about the undefinable connection between them; neither of them was ready to walk away from right now.

The door into the tube opened and a woman, one she remembered from his ship, left with a bag on her shoulder and another in her right hand. Amber. *The bitch who doesn't like me.* She glanced Corina's way, her gaze narrowing as she lifted her head and pushed back her shoulders. For one long moment, they stood, gazes locked before the other woman finally turned and walked away down the corridor.

A thousand unspoken words past between them and whatever the fight had been, whatever the problem, it was over and done with. Amber would no longer be a part of David's life.

Leaving? Why was the woman heading off the ship? She'd seen enough men and women changing berths to know what was going on, but this was slightly different. The challenge was obvious and personal. *What the hell have I done to her? I know she doesn't like me but shit...*

She'd done nothing, except capture the attention of one man.

Oh shit. She wanted David. That's it, isn't it? She wanted David. It wasn't as if she'd walked back into David's life on purpose. If she had a problem, then Amber should have taken it up with David, not wasted her energy glaring at her. *Maybe she did, and it's why she's leaving the ship? Or perhaps she can't face the fact David's married? Fuck, I don't know if I could sit, waiting and watching a man I couldn't have.*

Corina rolled her eyes and put the incident behind her as she punched in the code to the access tube. It only took a moment before the door opened, allowing her to enter the tube and walk the short distance to the entrance hatch into the ship itself.

A hatch which remained closed as she approached it.

This is my last chance to change my mind and enjoy the time.

Corina stopped and took a deep breath. She wasn't the type to run away from a problem, hell she hadn't run before this entire thing with David, and she couldn't do it now. This man, this walking trouble, was a part of her life, and she had to make a decision. One which didn't include walking away.

She shook her head, took a deep breath, and tapped on the closed hatch.

Nothing happened. Okay, what the hell was going on here? She checked the time. Fine, was he trying to upset her by keeping her waiting out here or had he changed his mind?

She shifted her weight from one foot to the other. One more minute and she'd...

The hatch slid open and relief washed through her. Though she knew he wouldn't have changed his mind, the doubt had been present and had grown with each passing moment.

"Sorry, had a task to finish off, and it took longer than I planned," David explained as he stepped to one side and let Corina walk onto the ship. "I hope you weren't kept waiting too long?"

"No, I'm fine. The crew member who left?" No point in hiding it. "Amber, wasn't it?"

Last Name

"Yes. Amber's been with the ship a few years now, and we'll have to pick up a replacement at our next stopover. Right now, though, we can manage." He gave a slight smile and closed the hatch. "Doesn't matter — I mean it doesn't impact our time together or shouldn't. And I don't want you worrying about the work we do. This time is about us, nothing else."

Except his people, his ship now mattered to her. She wanted to know more, much more, about what had happened, and the way Amber had looked at her had spoken volumes. Still, this wasn't the time or place for it. "I'll take your word for it."

He held out one hand to her, giving her the option to take it. No, it was more than the offer of his hand, it was more. This was a chance to bury herself into his embrace, to lose herself in his touch and forget about their problems. After all, wasn't that what this time had been all about?

Dealing with him, with what they had, wasn't going to be easy, and a part of her wanted to turn and run. No. She had to see this through and take what was offered, yet all she could do was stare at the extended hand.

So, take it already.

Nervously she slipped her hand into his and let him tug her close. This was dumb, she shouldn't be this nervous. What was she? An innocent? A virgin who had never been kissed? Gods, this was nuts. The last thing she was — was a virgin. She'd lost claim to that before she'd ever left Gaea yet here she was trembling like a damn leaf.

He smoothed one hand over her hair. "Thank you for agreeing to this. It's what we both need. I know this couldn't have been easy for you."

She leaned into his touch, letting her eyes close for a moment. "I'm not taking you away from anything important, am I?" *And if I am, why it would matter? We both want this. Need this.*

"No. What about you?" He rubbed his thumb slowly down the length of her jaw. "Have you been cleared for duty tomorrow? I don't want you here if you're not entirely strong enough to…"

"Yeah, Piotr wasn't happy, but he found nothing in my system. The notes your medic provided were enough to quiet most of his nerves, but he still wants a follow-up check in a few days." Piotr had freaked, in his own, quiet, calm way. If he'd been able to pull it off, he'd have isolated her and run a million tests before granting her permission to return to duty.

Yet Piotr had been forced to clear her for duty, though she was under strict instructions to check in with him daily for the next week to make sure there was nothing else going on. She'd put up with it, keep her comments to herself and get on with her life.

"If I know you, then there's more to this than you're willing to tell me right now. But I'm not going to ruin our time together." David sighed.

Plenty of time for that later. They'd argue or discuss one topic too many, and it would devolve into a fight.

Stop it.

"Are we going to stand here for the rest of the day?" She glanced down the corridor. No one else was around, but then again, the ship was a small one, with a limited crew. No doubt they were all busy, especially as they'd lost one crew member.

David smiled, turned, and led her through the ship. She remembered the layout from her previous visit but a lot of it had been blurred, and her focus had been on other things when she'd left the ship.

Too many other things to count.

"You're distracted…" He stopped outside of a closed door.

"A lot going on right now. I'm sure you can understand, especially after the poisoning. I've no idea who was behind it, not yet at least but I'll find out." Hell, she would be back on duty tomorrow morning. Kraven would assign her to a duty post for when the prisoner exchange took place. Exactly what that would be she didn't know, nor did she care right now, but she'd be back at work and be able to focus on her duties. Where she wouldn't have to think about David or the limited amount of time they would have together.

He moved behind her as the door opened, sliding one had back and forth across her shoulders. "Let's see if we can remove those thoughts for now and focus on us."

Easier said than done.

She tensed, uncertain of what she should do. Oh, she'd come here with the intension of going into his room and enjoying herself, but now she could see into his room the doubt crept back into her mind.

"Corina?" He leaned in close, nibbling the back of her neck.

Shivers ran through her body, and she closed her eyes, sighing in delight. Her nipples peaked beneath her clothing, pressing against the fabric until they ached for his touch. Or hers. Either would have helped.

"Are we going to start out here, where everyone can see us?" His teeth scraped, lightly, over her skin.

"No...," she murmured and took a step into his room. She shivered and tried to keep her mind in order, but all she wanted to do was sink into his arms. The passage of his teeth across her skin was only the beginning, and her mind was all too willing to fill in the details of what would be waiting for her.

He followed the door closing behind him with a soft swish. "I didn't want to deal with the questions which would have raised, and we've got a few things we need to discuss first."

Did they know about the relationship? *Does it matter?* "Hmm, bad for morale?" She turned to face him and slid her arms about his neck. "Or would they think it was a free for all? With me as the prize?"

"With this crew, it's a coin flip, but we need to talk first. I don't want to push this back any further."

Here it comes. The excuse. Corina tried to push those ideas to the back of her mind, but they clamored for attention. "I'm listening."

David stepped back, out of her grasp. "I left because I was ordered to. I told you about my work, but the truth is I'm – shit – I'm breaking the rules telling you, but you need to know." He closed his eyes for a moment, taking a deep breath before continuing, meeting her gaze. "I'm a member of the Shadow Rangers."

Corina opened her mouth to speak, found her throat didn't want to work, swallowed and closed her lips, pressing them tightly together. How the hell was she supposed to deal with this? The Shadow Rangers were dangerous, they dealt with problems their own way and to hell with the consequences. Like the peacekeepers, they, supposedly, served the combined 'civilized' portion of space but unlike the peacekeepers they didn't always follow the laws of individual planets if they believed breaking them was for the 'greater good.'

"Corina?"

"I'm fine. I need a moment here." This answered more than a few questions but raised problems she hadn't thought about. "You were on assignment, and I was a part of it?"

"Yes and no. You became a part of my cover, you weren't a direct part of the assignment."

Okay, she could live with and actually understand his explanation. "I see."

"Do you?" His voice was gentle but filled with concern.

"Yes. No. Maybe. Gods, yeah, sure, the logical part of me gets it. You were under orders, but the rest of me needs time to process what this means."

He glanced toward the door. "If you need to leave, I'll understand."

"Shit no. I'm not going back on my word, David." She needed this time with him more than she could explain. "How long have you been with them?"

"Eight years. I can't give you more details, Corina. Gods alone know that I wish I could, but I'm already breaking the rules by telling you this much."

"I understand," she took a step forward and leaned in close, needing his touch. "Maybe one day we'll be in a position where you can tell me more." A lot more if she had her way.

"Maybe one day." He reached up, grasping the back of her neck to hold her close. "Gods, I've missed this."

She bit back a soft laugh. "It hasn't been that long." Heat pooled between her thighs, and she shuddered, trying to hold onto her sanity. He'd barely begun to touch her, and already her body was threatening to take control, to push her mind aside and jump on for the ride.

"It's been three years since you came to me completely willingly, love. Three long, horrible years." He tipped back her head and brushed her lips with his. "An eternity. Except I didn't realize how much I'd missed you until I saw you again."

Her eyes burned, tears threatening to spill down her cheeks. Her throat tightened, and she struggled to find the words. Did he mean it, truly mean it? Or were they nothing more than pretty words? She wanted to stop, make him answer a few questions before they continued.

Don't ask, don't risk it. Gods, for once enjoy what's on offer.

"Not enough time. It's never going to be enough time for us, David." The words escaped, pushed free by her heart as her mind screamed not to speak.

"We enjoy what we have, what time we have now, and deal with the fall out later." He pulled back enough so he could meet her eyes. "I don't want our time spoiled, love. I need this with you as badly as you now need it with me."

She was right in his arms. She'd always felt as if she belonged, and now she had a chance to find out what they meant to each other or if this was nothing more than another passing moment of pleasure.

More, it has to be more.

But what if it couldn't be? She knew the odds were far greater there would be nothing else between them but this final time together and – until this moment – she'd believed she could handle it, but now she wasn't sure.

I have to try.

His lips covered hers, tasting, claiming before he parted her lips with his tongue and delved into the soft, damp heat of her mouth. He groaned into the kiss, holding her close, and he became all too aware of his cock thickening beneath his pants. It throbbed with the need to be released from the confines of the cloth and thrust its way into her body until she cried out, sobbing beneath him.

Fuck, if I keep this up, I'll come before I have a chance to sink into her.

He hadn't done it since he'd been a boy and had no desire to repeat it today, or any other day. Not when she was here, in his arms, ready to spend this time with him and willing to make memories with him to see them through the long, dark months ahead.

"I need you. Now." She pulled free from the kiss long enough to speak. Her voice breathy, her pupils dilated. "Please."

"Not yet," no, he wasn't going to rush this. Better to move slowly and enjoy any time they had.

He pushed her back toward the small bed, making sure his door was locked. The last thing either of them needed was a member of the crew walking in on them. Sure, they knew he had company, but that wouldn't stop them if they were in the mood to cause a few problems. He cupped one breast, thumbing an erect nipple through her clothing. She groaned, her eyes half closing in delight. He smiled, claiming her lips again until they parted beneath his kiss. Gods, the taste of her lips was enough to send his cock hammering through his pants. Shit, he had to keep things under control before he pushed her over the bed and took her without care for her desires.

"David…" she whispered, breaking the kiss. "I need…"

"No, not yet." In control, he'd remain in control no matter what it took. "I'm going to make this special for both of us."

"How?" Her voice breathy.

"Trust me." He took a step closer to the bed and reached for the buttons on her shirt. Odd, she'd never liked snaps or seals though they were far more common. She loved the old fashioned feel of buttons. And so did he.

"I'm trying to." She admitted and closed her eyes, trembling beneath his touch.

The first button slipped free of the hole, baring the soft, pale flesh beneath. He leaned in and kissed the newly exposed skin, tracing the tip of his tongue over it. Salt mixed on his taste buds, combined with the delicious taste which was unique to Corina.

"Gods above and below…" she groaned, arching beneath the path of his tongue.

He smiled and opened the second button, licking a path slowly down her chest. The third button revealed the upper curves of her breasts, and he teased the taut swell of flesh exposed to his touch. Her nipples were hard, he could see through the cloth covering her breasts. It would have been easy to bare them with a tug on her clothing, but he wanted – needed – to take things slowly.

Seduction and romance.

A woman such as Corina deserved to be courted if she was his wife in every sense of the word. Or perhaps because she was his wife that such a courting truly mattered. He smiled at the idea. His woman. His wife. He would teach her the meaning of passion, the passion which could rule them both as long as he didn't lose complete control.

Yes, he'd give her the romance her soul cried out for. *As long as the romance came with a healthy dose of control, dominance, and understanding, he was in charge of the situation.* He bit back a sigh and tried to force the idea from his mind. If he wasn't careful, he would push her too far, and by doing so, he would gain nothing from the situation except an upset woman. Unless he was careful with how far he pushed things with her...

"David?" Corina murmured, her voice soft and breathy. "Are you there? Are you with me? I think I lost you for a moment."

"I'm fine, I'm here. It's fine, love." He smiled and leaned in to kiss the soft patch of exposed skin. His smile deepened as she shivered beneath his touch. Yes, he could find a way of balancing both needs. All he had to do was be careful with his choices then he would be able to show her exactly what she'd been missing since he'd walked out of her life.

He swirled the tip of his tongue over her skin, inching down, baring her breasts to his touch and gaze alike with a sensual slowness he hoped would lull her into a sense of peace. He had to time this correctly, push at the right time or it would come back to bite him hard.

Her left nipple peaked beneath the cloth of her bra, but he ignored it and opened the rest of the fastenings on her shirt before he tugged it off and let the material slide down to the floor. He barely lifted his lips from her skin, only enough to skim past her bra and down to the taut, sculpted form of her abdomen.

She groaned, arching beneath him, wriggling as her fingers clenched and unclenched, nails digging into her own palms as he teased a path around her belly button and edged toward her waistband.

Had she left marks? He growled and reached for one of her hands, forcing it open the next time she clenched. "Don't."

"What?" She gasped, tensing beneath his touch.

"Don't hurt yourself," he let go of her hand. "Please."

"I wasn't... but all right." She relaxed once more. "I won't."

He opened the fastening on her pants, nibbling along her skin above the waistband. How much longer could he keep himself under control? He wasn't sure, but with the way his cock threatened to punch through his pants, it wouldn't be much longer.

Hold on. He had to hold on.

David clenched his jaw, focusing before he continued. Licking slowly over the expanse of bared skin. His teeth were next, a soft scrape, the promise of more to come, and the rise of gooseflesh beneath his touch. The low moan slipped free told him he was on the right track. With a grin he continued, nibbling and licking over her body, tasting the salt coating her skin.

"David, please… I can't…" She groaned, wriggling beneath him.

"You can't what?" He teased and tugged her pants down, leaving only her panties and bra covering her taut form. Oh, there was so much more he could do to her. "Talk to me, Corina. Tell me what you want."

"Wait any longer for you. I-I need this. Please, do it." She panted, arching, wriggling beneath him, her words coming in breathy gasps.

"Do what?" He grazed his teeth along her inner thigh, her pants now on the floor with her shirt. The scent of her arousal filled his nostrils, and he inhaled deeply, savoring it. She was close, very close to breaking point. If he could keep control long enough. Now the need to take her, to feel her sweet body clench around his cock, was more than he could ignore. "What is it you want me to do?"

"Make love to me," she groaned.

"Is that what you want?" This would be the telling point. Did she want it soft, gentle, and filled with romance, or did she want their time to be rough and filled with raw passion? He had to know the truth.

"No… I want… I want you to fuck me." She gasped, the words forced between clenched teeth. "Please, fuck me. I'm begging you, love, fuck me until I can't think. Until I can't breathe. Until I'm yours and yours alone."

The words he'd needed to hear, and they set him free.

Chapter Ten

Corina gasped as he stepped back from her, leaving her shuddering, trying to catch her own breath. Had she made a mistake? Had he changed his mind about what they were going to do? What had she said to trigger this change?

She blinked and tried to focus, attempted to form the words which would give her the chance to question what was happening, but before she was able to put her mind back into order, he moved again. Strong hands grasped her by the waist and lifted her up over his shoulder. She struggled, trying to figure out what was happening as he thrust her down on her belly on the bed and grabbed hold of her panties.

"David." She protested.

"No, you wanted this, you'll get this." He yanked down, tearing through the cloth before he cast the tattered shreds aside.

She cried out, twisting, trying to turn onto her back so she could at least see what he was doing, but a hand pressed down between her shoulder blades, holding her firmly to the bed.

"What are you doing?" She protested and tried to look back at him over her shoulder. "Please, I..."

"You what? Changed your mind?" He leaned down and nipped at the back of her neck, his voice firm but calm. "Is that what's going on? You say one thing then want another?"

Corina shook her head. She wasn't sure what she wanted to do right now. Pain and fear combined for a brief moment until her inner walls clenched. Gods above and below, she wanted this no matter how brutal it might appear at first.

"You're mine," he lifted her up but only long enough to position her backside, so it was raised before he settled in behind her.

Yes. "No, I'm not." Where the words she gasped instead of the one word, her heart screamed at her to say. She tensed as the head of his cock press between her folds, knowing what would come next and knowing this is what she wanted despite the fear which threatened to take control. "I belong to no man. I'm — I'm free to…"

"That's where you're wrong, you belong to me, my love." His fingers tightened on her hips. "You have to know it's how it's meant to be or you wouldn't have agreed to this. You'd be telling me to stop, telling me enough, but you're not doing any of that, are you?"

Her throat tightened. Gods. He was right. She could stop this, all she had to do was speak out. Why couldn't she say it?

Because it would be a lie, and it's time to stop lying to myself.

"Do you want to stop?" He paused, the head of his cock nudging against the slick entrance to her heated pussy.

"No," she admitted, her voice soft. "I don't."

"I don't want to either," he thrust, fully, into her clenching heat, his fingers digging into her hips to hold her in place.

She tensed, her body tightening around his thick cock. Gods, she'd missed this. Missed the way he felt inside her. She groaned, moving slowly beneath him, her body adjusting to his width and the weight of him. Slick heat rippled through her core, clenching and releasing on his erection.

He pulled back, leaving only the tip of his cock between her nether lips. Corina shuddered, ready to move, to push back, but the grip he held on her prevented her from moving. "Please, I need to move."

"No, you need to hold still and let this happen. You need to let your walls down and see where this will take you. Take us." He growled behind her and thrust again.

She gasped and moved under him, her hips rolling as she pressed to meet his movements. Without thinking, she closed her eyes and let it happen. Let the pleasure and pressure of the moment move through her. Invisible but real, the connection reached between them, and it took a moment before she realized it was his finger. She whimpered, shuddering at his touch only to stop when his fingers moved away. A moment later, something touched between her buttocks.

The same fingers?

Slick and warm he pressed them, working one finger at first, against the tight, dark star of her anus.

No, he can't.

She opened her mouth to speak, but a fresh thrust of his cock prevented her from protesting, turning the sound into a low moan of delight. Only when the new spasm had worked through her body did she realize the pressure had increased between her buttocks. Slowly, in time to his thrusts, David worked his finger into her body. The pressure hurt at first, a small amount of pain, enough to leave her tense and shaking, but then it eased, turning the pressure into pleasure with each gradually deepening probe of his slick finger.

"We've never done this, have we? Even in our earlier times together, I think we're long past due, don't you?" He thrust his finger fully into her bottom in time with a deep thrust of his thick cock into her clenching, wet core.

"David." She gasped, shaking her head. She should stop this. Say the words needed to change his mind, but she was enjoying this far too much. "Gods, David."

"Hold on. I need to make sure you're ready for me." He nipped her left ear lobe and pressed a second finger in, joining the first deep inside her body.

She groaned, bucking under him. Her inner walls clenched and spasmed around his erection, but he wasn't done with her yet. He wasn't willing to let her down and simply allow her to come, relax and curl up with him.

"A little more work, don't you think?" Two fingers moved and played inside the tight confines of her ass, stretching her, preparing her for what was to come. "You're almost there, lover. Ready for this, aren't you?"

Ready? No, how could she be? Her body tensed before the next wave hit her. Pain and pleasure mingled within her core, pushing her closer to the edge, pushing her until she sobbed with delight, fighting to hold onto her sanity.

"Yes," he slid out of her pussy, repositioning himself until the head of his cock rested against her anus. "You're ready, lover. I know you are, but I need to hear you say it. I need to hear you admit it."

No, I'm not. But the words remained trapped behind her lips. Her body betrayed her, lifting and arching her hips until she pressed back, fully, against the engorged head of his cock. *I want this... Gods, forgive me, but I want this. I want this with him. I'm safe with him.*

"Tell me you're ready," he whispered close to her ear.

"Please, David, Gods, don't make me wait." She pleaded. *I shouldn't have said that. I should have told him no.* What was she doing?

He pushed, slowly, into her body, stretching her body, forcing it to adjust to his cock. She whimpered beneath him, trying to deny the pleasure combined with discomfort and small points of pain as he filled her. She tensed, shuddering under him, wanting to pull away but the pleasure overcame the pain, and she slowly relaxed, settling into the friction and sensation he offered her.

"Yes. Give into this. Let it roll through you love," he growled behind her, slowly moving in and out of her tight body. "Submit, this once truly submit to me, to this, to what we want."

Gods, how she wanted to, but could she live with the consequences of her choice?

Yes, yes, a thousand times, yes.

She whimpered and clutched the bedding beneath her, arching her back and lifting her body to him, moving with each slow, deliberate thrust.

"Let it go. Let it happen. Your body knows what to do."

What other choice did she have when her body was all too

willing to betray her. Entirely too happy to let him dominate her when she knew better than to allow this to happen.

"David, let me - oh gods..." she cried out, tightening around him. Her body burned. The need to surrender, to relax and submit to him, was overpowering, and she could no longer fight it.

She no longer wanted to fight it. She moaned, closing her eyes fully and letting it happen. Her body pulsed around his cock, shuddering with waves of pleasure rippled through her core and ass alike. This was what she had needed. This is what she had wanted from the moment they had met. He was the answer. He was the calm in the maelstrom.

Pressure built deep inside her core, threatening to strip her of her sanity and she sobbed. She arched, moving for him. Her body ready to surrender everything she was or ever would be as long as she didn't have to give up this moment with him.

David paused for a moment, giving her the chance to catch her breath before he moved again. He thrust. Hard. The pressure more than she could stand. She sobbed, moving beneath him. Arching. Clenching. Shuddering as it pushed her over the edge. Drove her to the brink...

"David." She screamed, surrendering to him.

"Mine. You are mine." He growled, drawing back one last time before he thrust into her, releasing his seed into the slick confines of her body and sending her over the edge and into the welcoming embrace of oblivion.

David smiled as she shuddered beneath him, her body wracked with tiny spasms as she passed out. It wouldn't be long before she awoke again, but at this moment, this brief moment, he could enjoy the feeling of her relaxing in his arms. He didn't want to move away from her or withdraw from her body, but he knew he'd have to soon enough.

He knew he'd have to face the questions and the doubt which

would flash across her eyes if she didn't give them a voice. How such a strong woman could have this many doubts when it came to how she felt about a man or what she wanted in a relationship, was beyond him. But perhaps it was her heritage, being torn between two completely different cultures that caused the problem?

And maybe one day he'd find the courage to ask her.

He sighed and slowly eased his still semi-hard cock free from her body. They'd have to shower when she awoke. Shower and no doubt talk, avoiding the topics they both needed to discuss the most, but it was how things worked.

Wasn't it?

"David?" Corina murmured and snuggled in closer until he wrapped one arm around her waist.

"I'm here," he nuzzled the back of her neck.

"I wasn't sure if you'd stay, not after you'd gotten what you wanted," she murmured, still half asleep.

What he wanted? Oh gods, she still didn't get it. Didn't understand what he wanted was her. At his side. For all time. How much more did he have to do to prove it to her? Perhaps the kidnapping was the only way it would sink in for her? It was a part of her father's traditions, or rather his people's, it was a chance he had to take. It would also help him fulfill his vows was another, if smaller, consideration he had to think about.

"I wasn't sure I'd enjoy it, but you surprised me." She admitted and turned slowly in his arms to face him. "Surprised both of us, perhaps? Or were you expecting me to – to be like that?"

"No, it wasn't a surprise for me." No point in lying. "You've always had a slight submissive streak with me, Corina. You needed the right moment to let it out, fully, instead of those tiny glimpses you've let me see in the past." He'd seen more than the occasional hint. It had always been there, waiting for the right man. Waiting for him to be strong enough to force her to see it.

Corina tensed, a low growl forming in the back of her throat, "submissive is the last thing I am."

"Corina, I'm not trying to insult you, I'm honest about what I see in you." Maybe he shouldn't have said anything. It wasn't as if he was trying to insult the woman. "Damnit, why can't you take it for the compliment it actually was?"

"Compliment? You're kidding me, right?" She growled and moved out of his arms and out of bed, taking the bedding with her. "You seriously expect me to believe that telling me I'm weak is a compliment?" She tucked the sheet in around her body and discarded the rest of the bedding before she glared at him.

"Weak? I didn't call you weak." He sighed and sat up. So much for their time together. If she kept this up, he'd be lucky to escape without being slugged. Maybe she'd been searching for a reason to fight, to spoil things between them then she'd have a reason to say why a relationship between them simply wouldn't work?

Being submissive wasn't the same thing as being weak. What would it take before she would finally see the truth? Before she'd realize letting her walls down with the right person could be a wonderful experience?

"You called me submissive; it's the same damn thing. I'm a warrior you son of an Ontorian whore."

With a low snarl, he pushed to his feet and stalked toward her. "That. Is. Enough."

She blinked and took a step back. "I'm not submissive, got it? Apologize, now."

"Like hell, I will. Yes, you are submissive in the right circomestances and with the right person. And there's nothing weak or wrong about it." He moved toward her, backing her into a corner, his voice a low, cold whisper. "It's a part of who you are. The sooner you accept it, the sooner you can learn to use it instead of letting it be used against you by your own damned fears."

Corina swallowed hard and straightened herself up. "We don't agree, nor will we ever. As such, it would be best if I simply got dressed and left. We had our time together, and it's now over."

"No," this wasn't happening. She wasn't going to walk out on him. "It's not over."

"What did you just say?" She clutched at the sheet and glared at him.

"I said no. You're not leaving. Not yet, at least. Not until we've sorted a few things out." He walked over to the door and punched in a security code, making it impossible for her to leave unless the same code was used to then open the door.

"You arrogant son of a bitch. You have no right to..."

"I have every right. One, this is my ship. Two, you're my wife. Three, I've already proved when it comes to the two of us, I'm the dominant one in the relationship." He turned and glanced back at her. "And we agreed to this one night, and it's not over. One night and you want to use any excuse you can to leave. It's not happening. There's a shower if you want to get cleaned up you're welcome to. Then we can talk, or go for round two, I'm open to either suggestion." His cock twitched putting its vote in for round two, three and four.

"If you think I'd get back in bed with you any time soon, you're insane." She snapped, her hands fisted in the sheet. "You - you betrayed me."

"Betrayed you? With what? Enjoying your body? Making you come? Having you sobbing and screaming under me?" He took a step toward her before he stopped and shook his head. "Go and shower then we'll talk."

"No talking. I'm showering, and you're unlocking the door, and I'm going home." She lifted her chin and glared at him. "Is that clear?"

Now she'd gone too far. With a low growl, he stalked across the room, hands clenching at his sides. "This is my ship. I'm the Captain here, not you. It means you don't get to give me orders. Not in play, not in reality and not in these damned quarters."

"I'm not a member of your crew, damnit." She took a step back though, her gaze wary.

"No, but while you're on my ship, you'll at least treat me with respect due my rank, Corina. I love you, and that's not going to change. I've always loved you, but it doesn't give you the right to walk all over me. And if I've got to spend the rest of the night teaching you respect, then so be it."

She swallowed hard then straightened her shoulders. "You called me weak and I..."

He sighed and shook his head, the tension bleeding from his body. "No love, I called you submissive, we've been over this already. A strong warrior might be submissive to another, and I've never doubted not for a second that you're a strong warrior. What's so wrong about enjoying a small submissive streak with the man you trust?" She had to see sense, if she didn't this was all going to hell in a handbasket with no way of salvaging the situation for either of them.

Her damnable stubborn streak wouldn't let go of the idea being submissive was wrong, or an insult.

"Except I don't trust you." She closed her eyes and folded her arms under her breasts, her voice soft and trembling. "How can I when you've walked out on me once before, and we both know you're going to walk out on me again any day now. Hell, for all I know you're leaving once I depart your ship. Your work will always come ahead of any woman you're involved with, and it means you'll lie to them, hide things, cheat if you have to, and steal to keep your oath to whichever services you're working for these days. It's simply the nature of the beast." She opened her eyes and met his gaze, her eyes glimmering with unshed tears. "I know this is how it will be with you. I know it because in my own way I'm the same. I gave my oath to the peacekeeper service, and I won't back down. I can't break it without destroying a part of myself and being released from my oath is the one I won't ask for without a damn good reason."

It was finally all out in the open, the understanding they were cut from the same cloth, and neither of them would walk away from the careers they'd built for themselves. It wasn't in their nature to give up and walk away from a lifetime of work.

Chapter Eleven

Corina struggled to keep her emotions under control as she walked into the bathroom and closed the door. This had been a mistake of epic proportions. If he didn't let her leave when she was done with her shower, she wasn't sure what she was going to do. He was right on one thing; he was the captain, and ordering him around wasn't going to work. At least not in his quarters or anywhere else on his ship.

I could ask.

As if it would work. Besides, if she did, he'd never let her forget it. He might say it was another sign of the phantom submissive side he wanted to push with her. With a groan, she turned on the shower and hung up the sheet she had snagged from his bed. She'd made mistake after mistake, after mistake with him. When would she learn the best thing for her was to keep her distance from men? Especially from this man.

What was she supposed to do?

Shower, redress and persuade him to open the door so she could leave the ship and return to her quarters. She had, after all, enough to keep her busy for some time to come. But it would mean walking away from him and their last time together. She wasn't sure she was ready to do. Not without tasting him again. Not without letting the walls down fully and merely enjoying, the way she had earlier.

Weakness.

Isn't that what her father's people would call it? Or was he right? Did a warrior submit to another warrior? She vaguely recalled a detail or two about it from her studies, but such was a private matter between mates or done because of a bride kidnapping, or a groom kidnapping.

She smiled at the idea of snatching David and bending him to her will. It would be delicious to control him. Have him willing and gentle, obedient, and pliant to her whims. Gods, not that he'd ever bend in such a manner. It wasn't like him. She'd never seen a glimmer of submission in him, but being honest he was right, it existed in her when she was with him. And hiding from the truth, lying, becoming angry, wasn't going to change a damn thing.

She leaned against the sink and stared into the small mirror. A flush across her cheeks, the type left by mind-blowing sex. Mind-blowing sex and she wasn't going to deny they'd shared such a moment — several long minutes — of orgasmic, screaming sex.

Where did that leave her?

Same place she'd been before she'd stepped onto his ship. One night and it was over, then why was she trying to rush through the time when this was all there would ever be between them? When this might be the last time she would ever see him?

Because I'm a fool. A proud, stubborn, angry fool.

Shower, calm down time then she could face him again. Face him and face herself, everything about herself then they could enjoy this time together and finally find a moment of peace between them. A moment they could take and use during the dark times which lay ahead of them. After all, when you lived and worked on Freedom Station, you didn't know when your last moment might be, or when the war would fully erupt between the twin planets in the system.

Twenty minutes later, Corina stepped out from the shower and dried off. The woman who stared back at her from the mirror was a far calmer version of the one she had seen before the shower. Now, at least, she should be able to face David and work things through with him, and maybe she could bury her own pride and apologize to the man.

She finger combed her hair and straightened her back, checking the mirror one last time. When had she been this damned concerned about her appearance? This was a new aspect to her nature she wasn't sure about. After all, what did it matter if she looked messy or not? She wasn't an Adept of the temple of Gaea who needed to be pleasing in all things. No, she was of the line of Mars... and Gaea no matter if she wanted to ignore the fact. She had no talent for healing, her calling would likely have been pleasure had she pushed her father's blood aside and given into her Gaean nature.

A nature her mother had been adamant would overpower anything from her father's bloodline.

Stalling for time, coming up with excuses which would prevent her from stepping outside and facing David again. A coward's act and she was no coward. She took a deep breath, pushed back her shoulders, wrapped the sheet around her body like a toga, and stepped outside.

David lay on the bed, eyes closed, one hand behind his head. His gloriously naked body stretched out for her entertainment. She swallowed hard and tried to turn away from him, but her mind had other ideas. She couldn't turn away. Her gaze played down the length of his exposed flesh, lingering on his lips before trailing down his face to his chin and resting on his chest. Small curls of dark hair decorated the sculpted tones of his chest. A few small scars she hadn't noticed before. One carved a path under the left-hand side of his ribs, thin and long.

A knife, or a laser blade? Either could have stolen his life by the appearance of the long-healed wound. It had been deep. Fuck. She could have lost him and never known how he felt about her.

When had it happened?

She frowned, spotting a few smaller marks on his chest before she let her gaze move slowly down to his waist before it followed the trail of hair down to his groin. His cock, semi-flaccid, lay along his thigh, nestled in a patch of curls which tempted her fingers. Like this, her body moistened with the need to touch him again, to be affected by him, but it wouldn't solve anything between them.

This time together isn't about healing things or coming up with an answer. It's about pleasure. Shared pleasure. Time together. Nothing more. Got it?

Last Name

Her gaze fixed on his cock as it twitched under her gaze. Oh yeah, she got it all right. No denying what they could do together, and her body tingled with the memory of what they had recently enjoyed.

"Like what you see?" His voice, rich and deep, pierced her thoughts.

"Always, but you knew that already, didn't you?" She admitted and sat down in a chair a few feet away from the bed.

"Yes, but a guy likes to know these things." He opened his eyes and sat up, frowning at her choice of locations. "Feeling any better?"

Okay, here it was. "Yes... and I'm sorry. You're right. Submission between ma - lovers isn't a weakness, I understand what you were saying. I'm not used to admitting that side of me exists and it was a shock to be confronted with it."

Hmm, saying that didn't hurt. Not that she could speak the word mate. Not right now. Perhaps one day, when she finally got to the bottom of what lay between them but not now. He hadn't reacted to the change in word either. Maybe he hadn't noticed?

No, he knew. He had simply chosen not to say anything.

"I understand," he swung his legs over the side of the bed and sat up. "One of the things I've always loved about you was your strength and what I said to you, about you, wasn't meant to hurt. Only to get you to see the possibilities of who you can be with the right person." He sighed and lowered his head. "If the right person turns out to be someone else."

Her heart sank at his words. Was he serious about it? He was the right person for her. He'd always been that person, but their lives didn't match up. "Where do we go from here, David? What should we do about all of this?"

"It's up to you. If you want to leave, then I'll open the door and let you go. I'll be here for another day, maybe two, depending on when the orders come in, but after that, I've no idea how long it will be before I'm back again. If you'll still be here. You could be shipped off to another post by the time I return." Only then did he lift his head and meet her gaze again. "It's how the job works for both of us."

Something was wrong. A piece of reality she couldn't put her finger on but for all she knew it could simply be the torrent of emotions threatened to get in the way of the time they had left. "Perhaps it would be best if I did leave, for now, I mean." They'd had sex, argued, made up, what else was left? She could leave, turn her back on him and go back to work.

"If that's what you want, I won't try and stop you."

Why wasn't he trying to persuade her to stay? Was it a case of he'd gotten what he wanted, and now he didn't need anything else from her? Her back stiffened. Gods, it would be just her luck this had been nothing more than a booty call, despite his words.

"You're working tomorrow, aren't you?" He leaned down and reached for his pants. "Isn't that what Kraven said, you'd be able to return to work tomorrow?"

"Yes, back on duty." He was getting dressed, which meant this was over. She only had herself to blame after the way she'd reacted to him. Fuck. What was she supposed to do now?

"I know you feel out of place when you're not allowed to work."

It was yet another reason why she couldn't walk out on her career. This kept her sane or as sane as she was ever going to be. "Kraven had every reason to suspend me after the stunt I pulled. I was lucky he didn't boot me off the station with a negative recommendation."

"You always were hot-headed, especially if a man wanted to judge you based on anything other than your skills."

"You've got things to do this evening?"

"There's always work I can do on the ship. The joys of being the captain, it means the work never ends." He fastened his pants and walked over to her, pulling her out of the chair and into his arms. Arms he then wrapped around her, holding her against his chest. "This isn't easy, letting you go. Shit, it's the hardest thing I've ever had to do." His voice rumbled in his chest, vibrating into her ear. The sound soothing. "But I know I have to let it happen."

She blinked, hard, trying to clear her vision. Tears. She was crying. This wasn't like her. She didn't cry. At least not where anyone else could see her. "It's for the best. You have your life, and I have mine. The rangers and the peacekeepers don't mix." She leaned into him, relaxing though her cheeks were now salt marked.

"Maybe. Or maybe we simply haven't spent enough time trying to figure out an alternative. One which would work for both of us." He smoothed one hand over her hair before he palmed the back of her head and tipped her face up.

"An alternative that doesn't exist, love."

He smiled, though it didn't reach his eyes. "It's the first time, I think you've called me love since we parted company."

Her heart missed a beat. "Yes, I guess it is."

"Do you want to leave?" He lowered his lips, meeting hers, brushing them softly with a caress left her tingling and wanting so much more than a single kiss.

No. She didn't want to, but she had to before she lost her strength of will and gave in to the insane voice inside her mind as it told her to stay. Stay with him forever, even if meant giving up on her career. "It would be best if I left, for now."

"Why?" His breath warm against her lips.

"Because if I don't leave now, I'm not sure I'll have the strength to later."

He smiled, his eyes sparkling. "Thank you."

She didn't need to ask for what.

Chapter Twelve

David fastened his belt in place, and double checked the time. An hour before he had to be in place, plenty of time to check he had the ship ready, his crew up to speed, and the route planned out. And a dozen things could still go wrong. The time he'd spent with Corina hadn't been long enough, but if it all worked out, she'd be in his life for years to come.

Unless, of course, it all went wrong to the nth degree and he ended up angering Corina to the point where she spent the rest of her life hunting him down. *Hey, at least she'd still be in my life, right?*

His final check-in had confirmed the time of the handover, which pinpointed when he had to snatch Corina. And there'd have to be enough witnesses to cause the chaos he needed. As long as he declared a bride kidnapping it fell under a matter of custom rather than law, but it would still push Kraven off balance and create the distraction needed for the other team to get his brother out of danger.

Corina could fight back before he managed to hit her with the stunner. The time of the hand over could change with no notice. A well-meaning friend might try and help Corina out then all hell would break loose. She might wake up before he could get her back to the ship. Kraven might decide he was lying about the kidnap rules and interfere.

Or the station could come under attack.

Focus on what can be dealt with. Not on what ifs. Easier said than done.

"Captain, we're all set here."

"I'll be leaving the ship shortly. Keep everyone on full alert. We need to be able to slip the berth within sixty seconds of me returning to the ship." That was cutting it fine, but for this to work, to appear as if he were doing nothing more than following the traditions of his people, he had to be able to get away from the station quickly. "Have you found out who, on Mars, we need to contact with the announcement? I need the information to hand when I return."

"Yes, sir. I have the connection preprogrammed in, ready for when you need it," the reply soothed his nerves. If things disintegrated on him, he'd have proof this was nothing more than a bride snatch.

Odd, when he'd gone over the basics of the plan with his people, no one had protested. No one had offered a saner method of reclaiming his bride. Or attempted to talk him out of it. There'd been a sideways glance from Shiel, but that had been it. He'd expected questions, or a mumbled comment about Amber's departure being tied into Corina's presence in his life, but it hadn't happened either. Whatever happened, he knew he had his team, his crew, behind him.

"Captain, engines are up to speed, and all stations are secure." The final report came in. "We're ready when you are."

"Got it. Leaving now." He closed down the link and headed for the door. If his calculations were correct, then Corina would be in the briefing with the rest of the team, being filled in on the details of the prisoner transfer.

She would be ready for anything except this.

Shit, he didn't know if he was ready for this, but he was going to go through with it regardless.

Stepping out from the docking tube and into the station, nothing out of place. Obviously, the transfer was being kept under wraps and considering the parties involved, it was safer. It wouldn't take much for the twin worlds to dissolve into full war once more, which was the very thing the station had been built to prevent.

David moved through the station at a steady pace, taking note of the positions of the peacekeepers, and which bars or businesses had extra security in place. After the fight, it didn't surprise him to see a few more hired hands sporting weapons, and he hoped they'd stay out of it when he grabbed Corina. Not all of the merchants liked her, from what he'd been able to find out, because of her tendency to shoot first and ask questions later. Respected, admired, but they didn't like, which was one thing in his favor.

"Captain, message from control. It's a go." The small voice informed him over the open communicator. "It's all down to you now."

"Understood." No turning back now.

Corina clasped her hands behind her back, listening to the report. A prisoner transfer? Not any old damned prisoner but a man who could turn this station upside down if it went wrong. It was going to make life interesting. Who they were handing the prisoner over to only added to the list of things which could go horribly wrong.

"Sir, this prisoner, why are they doing this on the station when he's obviously dangerous?" Brian, one of the newer transfers, inquired. "I mean, wouldn't it make more sense to do this elsewhere?"

"Because of the treaties which bind us on the station. We can't interfere even if we believe he should be turned over to his own people. They're able to swap him for whomever they wish." Kraven explained calmly from behind his desk. "What they do with him after the fact, isn't our concern."

Brian shook his head but didn't speak.

"What's wrong?" Kraven pressed.

Brian's words were clipped and sharp. "Nothing's wrong."

"No, there obviously is. Speak up and get it off your chest." Kraven sighed and gestured with his fingers. "Better to get it out in the open before it eats away at you."

The younger man frowned then nodded before he continued.

Last Name

"They'll kill him, sir. I mean, eventually, they'll kill him. Once they're done interrogating him."

"Maybe, but more likely they'll sentence him to the games. That's the norm, and he could live a couple of years before he finally falls in them, depending on how skilled the man is." Corina spoke in a clear, steady voice. "It's not about that though, it's not our choice, our laws in play here Brian."

"Corina's right. When you take the oath to serve on a station like Freedom Station, it means accepting there will be situations where you stand by and allow things that are obviously wrong, happen. If we get in the way here, we undo all the work the men and women on this station have achieved, and the eventual loss of life will be far greater than you or I can imagine." He pushed free of his chair and moved around his desk. "Those of the twin worlds are a bloodthirsty, angry group, of people. They hate each other with a passion can't be denied. Their very foundations are set so they can never be friends with their neighbors and this station prevents them from bombing the crap out of each other."

The ultimate battle of the sexes taken to an extreme. One no one should ever have to live through. Corina had never believed how bad it could be until she'd started work on the station. Then it had taken separating two opposing factions in a bar fight, one where an innocent bystander had been knifed before she'd come to terms with how bad it was.

"Can't they be made to stop, to take a break in their war?" Brian pressed, his voice wavering. "I mean we have the power, don't we? The Peacekeepers I mean?"

"No one has that power," Kraven spoke calmly.

Ah, to be young and full of hope. As far as the legends were concerned the battle between the twin worlds had begun long before either world had found a way to venture into space. Both had always subjugated one gender, and once they had realized there was another planet in their system, with sentient life forms, they'd fought to free their ruling gender from the cruel oppression of the opposite sex.

The first encounters had been violent. Later ones had resulted in planet to planet combat. Raids. Assassinations. Then it had turned nasty. Only the intercession of the peacekeepers and the building of the station had prevented the two worlds from wiping each other out once and for all. In a war where both sides had the power to destroy a planet, there could be no real winner; only mutual destruction.

The station, however, hadn't put an end to all of the raids, or the small digs at each other the citizens of the two worlds engaged in. Nor did it prevent the games, slavery, and brutality which continued.

"I don't understand. All they have to do is listen to what's going on. To the idiot mistakes, they're making. That's all. It's simple, isn't it?"

"No it's not, and they won't listen. You're asking two races to turn their backs on their beliefs. Short of a major miracle, it's never going to happen, our best bet is to simply deal with the situation as it affects those on the station." Kraven lifted his head and turned his attention to the assembled men and women. "I don't like this prisoner transfer any more than the rest of you. From what I've seen, this man isn't a citizen of either world, and I've no idea why the transfer was agreed to. But it's our job to make sure it happens without any problems."

The man, whoever he was, would end up in the games and eventually, he'd die. It would be bloody, messy, a death to amuse the crowds and they'd cheer as he spilled his blood on the sands. That was the end of the matter or should be, but as she glanced at the image of the prisoner, a nagging itch settled in on the back of her neck.

Something about the eyes felt familiar...

"A problem, Lieutenant Greenheart?" Kraven inquired.

"No, sir. Just - for a moment - I thought I recognized him. But I don't. He must have one of those faces." She shrugged it off.

Last Name

Whatever she'd seen it didn't matter. She, like the others in the squad, had a job to do.

"Harwood, take Brian and Liana to secure the dock. I want the area double checked and locked down." Kraven went through the duty list, assigning each man and women in the room to their post.

"Greenheart, I want you on the exterior door. I'll need your full attention, but I know I can trust you. No one gets in or out without going through you, got it?"

"Yes, sir." Guard duty, someone had to do it. Besides, she was capable of keeping her focus on whatever task he assigned to her. "Anything else, sir?"

"No, you're all dismissed to your duties."

David checked the time for the third time in ten minutes. She should have been here by now. Had the briefing run longer than expected? He frowned and tried to relax. Shit, he didn't know how he would explain to Corina how he'd found out where she'd been assigned. He should count himself lucky that command's hackers had been able to get the duty list before Corina would have been informed of her assignment for this situation. At least it had given him the chance to go over the plan and set himself in the right position to see when she arrived.

A movement caught his attention out of the corner of his eye. Corina.

She strode through the corridor, head held high, each step filled with purpose. Pride, determination, and concentration, but it didn't detract from her beauty or the sensuality he could see rippling through her body.

His cock tightened, and he forced his focus to other things. Images which didn't include the way she'd moved beneath him the previous night. Time later, once he had her on his ship, shackled and claimed her as his bride then kept out of her reach for the next three years in case she tried to kill him for it.

Shit, he still hadn't worked out exactly what to do if she reacted violently.

Corina took position outside of the door, and they both waited. David where he could see her; Corina at her post. Fifteen long minutes past before the advanced members of the exchange party arrived. His brother wouldn't be in this group, and there were only two members of the security staff. Okay, it was within parameters, and besides, he wasn't handling the extraction side of the equation.

Not this time at least.

He would be long gone before the extraction team arrived. Gone with Corina and ready to face her anger when she woke up.

She's going to kill me. And if she figures out the full reason behind the timing of the snatch, she's going to kill me, bring me back to life then kill me again as many times as the tech will force breath back into my battered body.

And he'd deserve it. After everything he'd pulled, the leaving, coming back, snatching her, she'd have every right to beat him to a bloody pulp, but it wouldn't stop him from going through with it. Not because he'd been ordered to but because it was the right thing to do if he wanted to keep Corina in his life.

No, I can't think like that. This is duty. Sure it was, it's why his cock was hard at the idea of kidnapping her...Focus. He had to focus if he wanted to pull this off. David closed his eyes for ten seconds, then opened them, watching her.

Time to move.

Only three other people in the corridor now the advanced team had entered the docking area. Civilians. It would make life easier. With a smile, he walked into view and stopped, nodding in her direction as if he'd only just spotted her.

Keep it gentle and natural. She has enough to watch for she shouldn't be concerned about me. About what I'm doing here. As long as I don't arouse her suspicions.

Last Name

Why would she be suspicious? He knew how to handle this. Then why was his heart pounding so loud she should be able to hear it?

She won't, keep your cool, you know what to do. She'll be fine with all of this – at least until it's too late to do anything about it.

"David?" Corina frowned as he approached. "What are you doing here?"

"Not your normal type of duty," he nodded toward the closed door behind her.

"I don't write the roster, I get on with whatever I'm assigned to do, a fact you should understand." Her gaze narrowed, her tone cold and business-like. "Anything you wanted? I'm working, and whatever it is, it can wait. Can't it?"

He winced. He deserved that, but it didn't stop it from hurting. "I'm heading out in a few hours, my orders came in sooner than I expected. I didn't want to leave without saying goodbye this time. I told you I'd let you know and I'm through with breaking promises to you."

Color seeped across her cheeks. "Thank you, but I can't – I'm working, duty; you understand."

"I do, but is it too much to ask for one, quick hug before I leave, or a kiss?"

"You're asking if you can cop a feel before you vanish on me again," she sighed, rolling her eyes. "Fuck. Your timing sucks."

"Hey, I'm a guy, and I believe I have a pulse so of course, I want to grab and squeeze if I get the chance for one," he grinned and shrugged, ducking his head slightly. He wasn't exactly lying.

"And I'm on duty." She pointed out calmly then sighed. "Fine, make it quick. I'm not going to risk a report so you can grab ass." She took a quick look around before she nodded he could come in close.

He felt guilty when he moved in for a quick embrace, but he pushed that to one side as her body pressed against his, her arms encircling his neck. It had to be done. He had to go through with this and fulfill his side of the mission.

"I'm going to miss you," she murmured. "I wish – wish things could have been different."

He didn't reply. He didn't dare. It took every ounce of self-control he had to focus on removing the pen injector from his pocket without her noticing. One chance, one shot, it's all he had for this.

"Are you coming back anytime soon?" She asked in a quiet voice.

"I don't know." Fuck this hurt. Her words lanced through him, but he brought up the pen and pressed it, quickly, against the back of her neck. "I'm sorry," he whispered as he hit the release.

She tensed in his grasp, jerking once but she didn't have the chance to make a sound as the short-term stun hit her system and she collapsed in his arms. David moved quickly, scooping Corina up and over his shoulder before turned and headed down the corridor. Drugs were a no go, but a stunner – that he could get away with.

"Hey, what the hell?" A member of station staff in maintenance uniform called out. "What do you think you're doing with that Peacekeeper?"

"Bride Kidnapping, per Mars traditions." He called back, hurrying along. The report would be called in, and chaos would follow. By tradition, only a member of her family, or father's clan, could interfere.

Thanks to the conversation they'd had David knew her father was dead, and he was sure there wasn't a member of her father's clan serving on the station. Unless she had an adopted line here, there wasn't a single man or woman who could step up to dispute the kidnapping.

With a grim smile, he ran for the docking tube connected to his ship. Five minutes, he had five minutes to get clear of the station if this was to work. He darted through the growing crowds, ignoring the comments and stares, barely making it to the tube on time. He keyed in the code and dashed through and onto the ship.

"Get us out of here, now." He called out, shutting the hatch behind him.

"On it, Captain," the reply was calm and collected, precisely what he expected from a member of his crew. Odd, he'd assumed this entire thing would be a lot harder...

Chapter Thirteen

Corina groaned and rolled out her shoulders, blinking in the dimly lit room. What the fuck had happened? She frowned, trying to figure out why she couldn't move, and why her mouth felt like it had been stuffed with week-old socks. What the fuck had happened to her? The last thing she could recall was standing, talking to David about...

David.

She growled and moved her left hand toward the back of her neck. She stopped, the subtle sound telling her that her wrists had been chained together then to the bunk or the floor. More likely, the floor with how she was laying. He'd drugged her. The idiot had stunned her.

Of all the arrogant, ignorant stunts to pull. What the hell did he think he was doing?

I'm going to kill him. Maybe she was, once she'd found out what was behind all of this.

No, I'm going to kill him. Slowly. After she'd fucked him one last time, or maybe two... okay three then she'd be done. She shook her head, trying to clear it. Whatever he'd used had done a number on her, but now she trusted him enough to know it wouldn't have caused any long-term damage to her system.

At least she hoped it wouldn't.

Her vision cleared slowly, but there was only one source of light in the room, close to the door, and it was dim at best. She wasn't in his room, more likely a part of the hold.

Or a cell. Her jaw tensed. He'd locked her in a bloody cell. Who did he think he was?

How long had she been in here anyway? Oh Gods, the prisoner exchange. He'd snatched her from her duty post, leaving it unguarded. If anything had gone wrong, it would be her fault for not being at her position. He couldn't have done this to her at the worst time. She was derelict in her duty, and Kraven would have her head if she screwed it all up.

Her stomach knotted.

"David, I know you can hear me, you bastard. Come down here and unchain me or so help me. I'll skin you alive." She screamed at the closed door then stared at the chains.

She wasn't on a bunk but on a thin mattress pad on the cold metal floor. *I suppose I'm to feel grateful he saw fit to give me the pad instead of leaving me on the bare floor.* It didn't improve her mood.

The chains were heavy duty, as were the manacles on her wrists and about her ankles. It took her staring at her feet to realize he'd removed her boots and socks, locking manacles around her ankles. Neither her wrists or ankles had more than four inches play between them, which was going to prove a problem soon enough. On top of that, there was a chain connecting her wrists to her ankles. The chain attached to a heavy D ring in the floor. She couldn't pull her way out of this one, and even if he hadn't stripped her of all weapons, tools and anything useful she might have been able to twist to her use, she'd have had a problem breaking through the chains.

Wonderful.

"Shit," she muttered and tried to sit up. Barely enough play in the chains to allow her the chance to move, and it took several minutes before she was able to complete the simple task.

Where they still docked?

She pressed her bare feet, carefully, to the cold metal floor. No, they were moving. Small vibrations betrayed the use of the engine made it clear they were no longer docked at Freedom Station. And, as she had no way of knowing how long she'd been out, she couldn't begin to guess at how far away they were, or what had happened in the time she'd been unconscious.

Frustrated, she tugged and pulled on the chains. Untold minutes of futile struggles led to sore patched on her wrists and ankles alike but did nothing to weaken the chains or the hold they had on her body. Which meant the only thing she could do was sit and wait.

Wait for David to show up, or a member of his crew, and find out exactly what was going on.

With a growl, she closed her eyes and tried to recall the mental disciplines her mother had wanted to teach her all those years ago.

David leaned back in his chair, waiting for the connection to complete. He'd done it. He'd actually done it without killing anyone. He'd honestly expected more problems in snatching Corina, but he wasn't going to complain about the lack of them.

"Monroe?" Blain's voice demanded his attention.

"Sir," he sat up, focusing on the conversation.

"We got him out. The distraction worked. You did your part exactly the way we needed, and the distraction worked perfectly."

Distraction. Corina was far more than a mere entertainment but no point arguing with Blain, he wasn't ready to listen. David let out a breath he hadn't been aware he'd been holding. His brother was safe, and with luck, he'd get the chance to find out exactly what his brother had been up to. "Was anyone hurt?"

"One fatality, a member of our team, but we retrieved the body along with our man. Kraven took him out. You were right about the man. Dangerous. Pity we can't recruit him for our teams. Still, at least we know his specific strengths now should we ever have to eliminate him. Now, your guest? Did you collect her without incident?"

"No fatalities." One dead. The nature of the beast and it could have been far, far worse. Kraven involved, he should have expected it. He was all too aware of how talented Kraven was, and he'd counted on those strengths prior to this incident. As for eliminating Kraven, it was a choice he would refuse to be a part of.

"She's secure in the holding cell. She's awake according to sensors, but I've been waiting to hear from you before I pay her a visit." He'd been using any excuse he could think of to avoid stepping into the room with her. The last thing he wanted, or needed, was to look her in the eyes right now. "I'll go into see her shortly."

"And will you let her go, or complete the kidnapping rite?" Blain inquired, his tone crisp and professional. "Either is fine by me." Blain paused for a moment. "Returning her would be for the best, I don't believe you have the time to balance your life with a wife in the mix."

The ultimate question. "I'm giving it thought, sir. If I don't go through with this, I'll be marked as a coward by her people, and it would give Kraven a justifiable reason to issue a warrant for my arrest." Not going through with it would also reduce his ability to work in many sectors.

"Ah, yes, of course. Agreed. I'm sure you're aware of other, potential, problems the choice might cause."

"Yes, sir." He paused, taking the time to phrase his next response carefully. "If I go through with it, and complete the rite, she and I will be married, completely, in the eyes of both Gaea and Mars. It means either I have to leave the service, sir. Or she has to leave her career. A hard decision on either end and not one I want to force her into." Not one he wanted to think too deeply about either, but the problem was he had to.

"I have faith in you to make the right decision. I'll be in contact in a few days when things have calmed down. Blain out." The connection severed, leaving David to think through what he had to do.

By rights, he should simply release her, but it would mean he would never, could never see her again. He hadn't lied to Blain about the problems if he didn't complete the rite, but there was also the issue of their careers. His heart told him to complete the ritual, his head said and find another way to keep his relationship alive and prevent Kraven from issuing a warrant. *Shit, this wasn't what I thought would happen.*

No, for some reason he'd assumed he'd be able to follow through with the rite without any hesitation. Claiming her for his bride would be the simple step following the dangerous one of kidnapping her from a busy station. Oddly enough, it had been far easier than he'd imagined. However, the idea of completing the rite had his guts in knots. It didn't matter how much he wanted this woman in his life if he failed, if he screwed this up, it would all be for nothing.

Get on with it already.

With a sigh, he pushed out of his chair and headed for the door. He knew what he had to do; he had to make himself do it.

He nodded to the only member of the crew he passed during his walk through the ship and down to the holding cell. It was another decision he would have to answer for. Locking her in a holding cell hadn't been his brightest move. Still, she was a trained peacekeeper and would have basic escape skills. That might have caused problems if he hadn't been fully aware of the training the woman would have received when it came to escape and evade. She'd no doubt tested the chains and manacles. Once she'd found she couldn't break or stress them, what would she have then done? He could have pulled up the security feed, but it would have been nothing more than a delaying tactic.

He stopped in front of the locked door and took a deep breath. She was still here. He straightened his shoulders and keyed in the code would open the door and raise the intensity of the lighting. He didn't want to blast her with light, not after so long in the dusk quality of the holding cell. Still, it was apparent the change caught her off guard as she was blinking hard and scowling when he walked into the room.

"Took you long enough, Monroe. I've been expecting you."

"Sorry, I was — busy with other things." A lame excuse and he knew it. Time? She had no way of knowing exactly how long she'd been held in the cell. No timepieces and he'd taken care to strip her of her personal equipment, including any means of tracking time. "You're well?" No, this wasn't the way to handle the situation. He took a step into the holding cell. The chains still held tight, as he'd expected they would.

"Angry, sore, and oh yes, did I mention pissed off?" She glared at him and lifted her chained wrists as far as the restraints would permit. "Get these off me. Now." She growled the final word, her gaze hard.

"Not until we've had the chance to talk," he hit a button, and a bench slid out of the wall wide enough for him to sit on without falling off. "Do you understand what I've done?"

"You snatched me, put my career at risk, and acted like a complete asshole locking me in a fucking holding cell, that's what you've done." She snarled at him, her hands clenched into tight fists. "What the hell else do I need to know unless it's when you're releasing me to return to work? If I have a job to go back to."

"No, it's more, Corina." He closed his eyes for a moment before he opened them and met her gaze. "I've started the bride kidnapping rite, and I intend to see it through. To the end, no matter what the outcome might be. It's why I didn't use a drug to knock you out but kept to the safer option of the stunner."

"Bridal kidnapping… shit." Corina opened her mouth, closed it, and swallowed hard before she finally spoke. "Tell me you're joking. This is a weird ass gag of yours, isn't it?"

"That would be a lie, and I've gone to too much trouble to set this up." He kept calm and watched her closely. "And I'm not about to back down now, not when this is all so close I can taste it."

"I'm not going through with this. No one pulls this kidnap and marry the bride shit anymore, it's a dead tradition and you can't make me do this. It's not been done in – fuck – a generation, maybe longer. You can't do this to me." She shook her head and glared down at her manacled wrists. "Do us both a favor and unchain me before this thing gets out of hand. I mean it, David. Get these chains off me."

He stood, slowly and moved toward her, staying out of reach of her chained hands. "That's where you're wrong, Corina. It's far from a dead tradition because over twenty bridal kidnappings took place in the last year on Mars. This tradition is still very much alive and kicking, and I intend to see this through to the end, no matter what the end might be."

Corina paled and shook her head. "No, you have to be wrong. I didn't hear about a single bridal kidnapping when I stayed on Mars. You can't be right." She all but stammered. "This isn't happening. This is a dream. A bad dream. I'm going to wake up from, and I'm in medical, injured and on a weird ass drug Piotr is trying out."

"I can show you the information myself. Each one, successful or otherwise, is registered with one of the temples. It's not made public knowledge, as in announced to the worlds at large, but anyone can check the records. I contacted the High Priest in the senior temple myself and let him know what I'd done. He explained the time limit to complete the rite and wished me luck." A non-Marian attempting the kidnapping was unheard of, and Corina's clan was a powerful one, known for strong, determined warriors. Corina herself had been through the training camps, and they were aware she was named and numbered amongst the warriors of Mars.

Which meant this could go wrong in more ways than he was ready to face.

"The High Priest took your call?" She ducked her head, her shoulders slumping in defeat. "Gods, this is real, isn't it? You're determined to go through with this. No matter what I think about this stupid situation you're going through with it."

"Yes, love... it is real." A band tightened around his heart. He'd chosen this path, and he'd follow it through. He lifted his head, straightening his shoulders before he continued. "Per the custom, I'm giving you notice that in two hours I'll return and we'll begin the rite, Corina Greenheart, daughter of Mars and Gaea." He placed one hand over his heart and bowed. "I hope you will enter into the rite with an open heart, and we both dare to accept the outcome, no matter what it might be."

The ritual words still echoed through her mind five minutes after David left her alone in the holding cell once more. He was going through with this. Actually going to make her go through the kidnapping right and he'd accept the outcome. The problem was, she'd also have to accept it, or denounce her bloodline.

This was insane. Whose fool idea had this been? She couldn't believe it was David's, and besides, he wasn't of Mars. How had he known about the tradition in the first place? It wasn't as if it was advertised off world. Who had planted this seed with him?

Whoever it was she planned on hunting them down and skinning them for shits and giggles.

Shit. She was in trouble here. She had the right of challenge. Just because he'd snatched her it didn't mean she had to meekly accept it, but she'd already lost one bout to him, and if she lost in a challenge match, she'd be bound to him as his submissive.

Did it matter? She acted submissive to him in the bedroom anyway, and she couldn't see him pushing matters outside of their private chamber. Either way, she'd have to follow his decision about the station; she wasn't happy about and denying her bloodline wasn't possible.

She could no more turn her back on Mars than she could turn her back on Gaea. Not without destroying a part of herself and that she wasn't willing to do.

Bloody stupid, barbaric, traditions.

He had no right to use them against her.

Actually, he does, that's the problem. He knows I'll honor the rite, I wouldn't turn my back on the clan – the family I still have.

She had to either accept the tradition as written, use the loophole, or denounce her bloodline. Option three was out of the question, which left only the first two, and the knotting in her stomach wasn't making it any easier to think the situation through.

Which setting had he used to knock her out? Whatever it was, the side effects would obviously be cleared from her system before the two-hour deadline. Completing the rite with her still woozy was against the rules.

At least Dad made sure I understood what the rules were, though I doubt he ever believed I'd be faced with following them through. Gods, what would he think about all of this? What would he tell me to do?

She growled, unable to rub her aching temples with the way he'd left her restrained.

Use the anger. Fight back. Go for broke. I might win.

No might. She would.

Even if I don't want to?

She scowled and closed her eyes, shifting so she could lean back against the bulkhead. He wanted her, perhaps loved her. A part of her screamed in joy at what he was doing. The bridal kidnapping was a declaration to the universe; this woman was the one you wanted above all others. The one you would protect with your last breath and each drop of blood in your body. The only woman in the universe for you. And he'd done it for her. Proclaimed his intention in a way so public it couldn't be denied.

How many had seen him lug her through the station? By now Kraven would know the full circumstances. David would have let the station know, if for no other reason than to prevent kidnapping charges being levied against him. No going back.

The rest of her growled at the chains and plotted revenge.

"Okay, this is how he's going to play it. Game. Fucking. On." She wasn't about to lie back and make it easy for him. No damned way. She was a warrior, and he was about to find out how dangerous loving a warrior could be. And if she lost, she'd do so with her honor intact and knowing he indeed was the right man for her. The consequences were ones she'd deal with later, and she would find a way to balance it all, no matter if it meant being told she had to walk away from her career.

Chapter Fourteen

Seeing Corina chained in the holding cell had been more than he could take. The image of her being helpless had done two things. Turned his cock rock hard, and knotted his stomach, but it was one thing to enjoy the submissive side to her nature, it was another entirely to keep her prisoner.

It would have been damned easy to strip her and enjoy her body.

It wouldn't have taken much effort to turn around, walk back into the cell.

Therein lay a problem. Facing the fact he was kinkier than he'd given himself credit for wasn't a detail he'd bargained for in all of this. If she accepted the rite as it stood, he would be dominant over her for the rest of her life, but at least he could keep it to the bedroom. Not that he had a problem with the bedroom aspect, but ordering Corina to leave the peacekeepers...

His jaw clenched. She'd never forgive him if he took that route. Where did it leave them?

A choice he'd never believed would be a part of his life.

"Captain, incoming from Freedom Station. It's Kraven, Captain."

David rubbed his temples for what had to be the hundredth time since he'd brought Corina onto the ship. "Patch him through."

It took only a moment before Kraven's voice rang out through over the channel. "Monroe. What the hell do you think you're doing? And don't give me your bride kidnapping crap. You didn't want a short-term relationship with Corina a few days ago, now you claim you want her in your life for eternity? Spin that line to one who doesn't know you." Each word a dagger threatening to slice through the lies he'd built around his life.

Okay, fine. He deserved it. "Maybe it's how I felt when we bumped into each other after the bar fight, but I've changed."

Last Name

That, at least, was honest. "I didn't know we were married until she told me, and I'm guessing you didn't know either or you'd have given me plenty of crap about it."

A moment's pause filled only by the soft crackle of interference or more likely Blain monitoring the communications. "Fair point, but shit, did you have to snatch her while she was on duty? You've no idea the number of problems you caused with your timing. You stirred up a real shit storm here. The only reason she's not facing charges is the fact you snatched her."

He knew exactly the problems he'd caused. "Sorry, I spotted an opportunity and took it. Nothing too serious, I hope. And I don't want her getting into trouble for a problem I caused, and it's a relief to hear she's not up on charges for something that isn't her fault."

"Yeah, I can't issue a warrant, stupid fucking custom prevents it. Like it should make a fucking difference when you walk into my station and steal one of my people. Shit. What made you dig that one out? I mean, fuck you could have asked her to marry you again if you wanted her in your life." Frustration poured through the channel.

"Yeah, and she'd have said no. She's committed to the service. This way, she doesn't have a choice."

"What the fuck has gotten into you?"

"She won't denounce her bloodline, you know her and I don't think I can live without her." The last sentence was softer. Words he'd mocked other men and women for. Words he'd sworn he never say himself as he was too strong to allow love to weaken him. "The idea of giving her up hurts as if I'm being cut with a blunt knife."

Words he now meant with each beat of his heart.

Kraven paused. "Shit, you've got it bad, man. Okay, fine, you've got a day to complete at most then I want to talk to Lt. Greenheart before anything else is done. I'm not about to lose one of my best officers without a fight." Kraven sighed, a low tapping sound ringing out. No doubt the man was drumming his fingers on the desk. "She's a good one, Monroe. Don't hurt her. And give thought to the consequences of your actions. She's not likely to take this lying down."

Yes, he did. Her spirit was one of the many things that had attracted him in their first meeting, and he had no cause to regret her spirit now. "I can give you this much, Kraven. She'll be free to talk with you once the rite is completed and I'll talk through the situation with her before I make a final decision about what's to be done about her posting on Freedom Station." It was the least he owed both Kraven and Corina, but would it be enough?

It would have to be.

"Thank you. Don't take it personally, but I won't wish you luck in all of this. Corina's a wonderful woman, and you might find out you've bitten off more than you can chew. Kraven out." The channel went dead.

More than he could chew? The warning neither surprised him, nor would it be the first time it had happened. But hell, at least this time he'd enjoy what led up to it.

Wouldn't he?

Corina lifted her gaze at the noise of the lock activated on the door. The tension had eased from her body in the time she'd been left alone in the small room, and she was ready for whatever he might throw at her. "Two hours, I presume?" She spoke calmly, lifting her gaze to meet his. "And I take it you'll at least allow me a few moments privacy with a bathroom before we begin this event? Or were you hoping to use that to your advantage?"

David frowned slightly and stepped into the holding cell. Obviously, whatever he'd been expecting from her it hadn't included calm, reasoned responses to his presence.

"Yeah, sorry. I hadn't thought about it." He paused for a moment, his hand moving to a control box on his belt. "Do I have your word you won't try to escape, Corina?"

She'd been ready for the question. "Yes, I swear by Mars and Gaea I will not attempt to escape until the matter of the rite has been settled once and for all. You have my word as a warrior and as a woman." She was one woman against a crew of, well, she didn't know how many were in his people, nor did she have the codes to get past any security measures his ship might have in place. Trying to escape at this point would have been a futile waste of energy.

No, better to save her energy for other more important things.

"Agreed," he lifted the box and activated it.

The manacles released from her wrists and ankles and a door opened up in the side of the holding cell, the light beyond revealing a small bathroom.

"I'll be a few minutes." She nodded her thanks and stood up before she walked calmly, and with as much dignity as she could muster under the circumstances, into the bathroom, closed the door and used the facilities. However long she'd been held in the cell it had been long enough for her bladder to start protesting, loudly.

After washing, staring into the small mirror, and finger combing her hair into a semblance of order, Corina left the scant privacy of the restroom and returned to the central portion of the holding cell.

"Thank you," she eased into parade rest, her gaze meeting his with a cool detachment. "Now, onto business."

David's jaw tightened. "Is that what this is to you? Simply business?"

"It's the best word for it at this moment in time, Captain Monroe." She allowed herself a small smile. "I didn't ask for this. I didn't ask to be yanked off the station, and if I let my emotions become involved in this, then I might kill you before we're through."

David's gaze narrowed, the muscles across his shoulders

tightening. "I claim the rite of the kidnapped bride, Corina Greenheart, do you willingly submit to the rite?"

She tipped her head to one side and counted - silently - to thirty before she answered. "I challenge your strength to hold me as your bride."

"What?" He took a step back. "Challenge? What the fuck?"

Hmm, maybe he hadn't known of the challenge? It was possible as it was rarer than the kidnapping. "I have the right as a warrior named and numbered by the Priests of Mars to challenge the kidnapper to single combat. Do you accept the challenge, or will you release me and your claim on me?" Of course, if he did release her, he'd be marked as a coward by her people, but he might not be aware. And he wasn't a coward, no matter what his decision today might be.

"This is a part of the rite I was aware of, but I don't have all the details, and I don't like making decisions without all the information, Corina. I need a few minutes to check on the details, will you grant me that?" His eyes had narrowed, but his voice remained calm.

She had the right to say no, but it wouldn't be fair to either of them. No, she had to do this the right way, no second-guessing later on, or accusations she'd tricked him. "Granted. But you don't lock me back in chains. I gave my word I won't try to escape, which means the chains are overkill."

"Agreed, however, I will have to lock the door," he smiled slightly. "You can't blame me for being over cautious. You are, at the end of the day, a Peacekeeper with all the training that goes hand in hand with your career path."

No, she couldn't blame him, but it didn't mean she had to like it. "Understood, though you should be able to take my oath as given. I've never broken an oath in my life."

David didn't move for several long minutes, "You'd do the same in my position, Corina."

"Maybe, but we'll never know." She settled back down on

the bench and folded her hands in her lap. "I'll be waiting for you when you get back, Captain Monroe."

The formal wording hit him hard. But she'd played her card, and all she had to do now was wait.

Fuck, this was a twist he hadn't expected. A challenge to the kidnapping? He had to research it one and fast. Sure he knew the basics as he'd said, but this required more knowledge. Five minutes of work turned up what he needed to know. The only one who was named and numbered amongst the warriors could pull the challenge, which was why Corina had used that particular phrasing. And as such women were seldom kidnapped, it meant the trial hadn't been issued, according to the records, in over a hundred years.

A hundred years and yet she was willing to chance it.

It shouldn't surprise me Corina would pull a trick like this either.

The more he read through about the challenge, the more interested he became. She was taking a risk with this if she lost, then her duty to him would be greater than it would be under normal kidnapping rules.

"Why would she do such a thing knowing the risk?" He mused and leaned back in the chair. He could see the appeal, if she won the challenge, then she'd be free of him, and he's still kept his honor and standing in the eyes of her people. Because she respected him enough to give him the chance to prove he was strong enough to take control, but she also knew Corina couldn't meekly submit to him.

He had to, in turn, respect her choice, but he also had to go through with it though he knew there was a chance he could fail. An equal opportunity she could lose, and if she did, there would be no escape from him at all, not the marriage or her submission to him. It would be compulsory, and only death would end the relationship no matter if he turned into a drunken, wife-beating asshole.

Marriage was one thing, but knowing divorce wasn't possible, no matter what happened between them, was a detail he hadn't considered.

The submission was another aspect to take into consideration. He liked her being submissive to him in the bedroom, but if this challenge ended in his favor, he could compel her all the way to chains and a collar. No, it wasn't in his nature, but there was a dark voice in the back of his mind, which found the idea of more intriguing.

Naked, crawling to my feet, willing to do whatever I wanted, whenever I want it.

How would she take it?

No, he couldn't think about it, yet the image returned. His Corina. Naked, chained at his feet. Wearing his collar. Fuck. He hadn't allowed himself to think about taking her submission that far. Not in the darkest recesses of his mind.

At least, I'm not willing to admit to it.

He swallowed hard and shook his head. Gods, what kind of man was he to think about putting her through it? It would destroy the woman he loved. No, bedroom play was one thing, her admitting and accepting he was in charge of their relationship was fine, but collaring her as his property?

Archaic.

Yet she'd known the risk when she demanded the challenge. Demanded it when she could have simply accepted the fact he'd kidnapped her and claimed her as his bride. At least then, if he'd become a monster, she'd have the right to return to her people. Of course, there'd be specific steps she'd have to take or her clan would, but she'd be able to leave.

She wouldn't have the chance if he won the challenge. It would be, as far as her freedom was concerned, be over for her.

Frowning, he pushed to his feet and stepped away from the

screen. The more the data had answered his questions, the more questions had arisen to plague him. He loved her. He wanted her in his life, but did he want so with her at his side or at his feet.

Why not both?

Gods, this was too much to think through clearly, but he had to take the time to figure it all out before he went back down to the holding cell and told her his decision.

Is there a decision to make? I kidnapped her, I know I want her in my life. I can't back down because she upped the stakes. Damnit, it's why she'd laid the challenge down in the first place, to see if I'd change my mind.

Smart woman but it didn't mean he liked what she was doing. A full-on challenge would make him either accept and find the courage, or back down knowing there would be no second chances for him on this. He couldn't argue with her decision, but it didn't mean he had to like it either.

Man up or back down those are the only two choices left.

He growled, turned off the screen, and stalked out of the room. If she wanted to challenge him, he'd take it up, and there would be no backing down now. She was his, and once this was over and done with, she'd be unable to deny it ever again. Corina Greenheart was his wife and would be in the eyes of both worlds before the end of the day. If he had to fight until he was ready to drop to prove the point, then that's what he intended to do.

He'd been gone for a while, but Corina was aware he'd need time to research the situation. Had she made a mistake in laying down the challenge? No, not a mistake but perhaps she hadn't thought through the situation entirely before laying the challenge down? She knew what would happen if she lost. Her life would change in ways she wasn't ready to deal with, but it didn't matter now. She'd made the offer, and she'd have to deal with the outcome.

She shrugged it off. Self-doubt, wonderful thing - not. She didn't have time for this. She'd made the right choice, and she would win the challenge. Once it was done, she could return to duty. She'd face questions from Kraven, and with just cause, but that wouldn't prevent her from returning to duty and serving out the rest of her term on the station, or being transferred to another post. She'd be able to handle either situation without a problem because this was what she'd signed up for at the end of the day.

Kraven will understand no matter what the outcome is.

The man knew about her past and had dealt with conflicts between traditions and the peacekeepers before now. Piotr had brought one of those to Kraven's office – in the form of his exiled sister, dealing with a bridal kidnapping turned challenge should be easy.

Uh huh, about as easy as keeping the peace between the twin worlds.

A small noise on the other side of the closed door caught her attention, and she sat up, watching for the first sign the door would open.

When it did she was ready, her hands folded in her lap, her expression schooled and her breathing steady. She didn't need a mirror to know her appearance, she'd practiced for many years. It was how you kept your enemies from knowing what was going through your head.

"Corina," he nodded and walked into the holding cell.

"Captain Monroe." She replied, watching him closely. He couldn't start the fight here, not enough room, not unless he folded the bunk away. No, realistically they needed space to move around. Would he think of that before starting or take advantage of the restrictive space? Fuck. He'd use the cell. With his larger frame, he'd have a distinct advantage, and he'd be a fool to ignore it. "I presume you've finished your research into all of this?"

"Yes, I have." He rested his weight evenly, but his stance was relaxed.

"And?"

"I accept your challenge," he admitted, his gaze never wavering. "Are you ready for the consequences of the challenge?"

"Yes, regardless of if I win or lose, I'm ready, Captain," she smiled slightly. She was as ready as she'd ever be. "Where and when?"

He closed his eyes for a moment, but when he opened them, they were emotionless. "Here and now. I know the space is cramped, but it will work. At least we won't be disturbed here."

There was something about the way he shifted his weight, the creasing of lines around his eyes. What was going on? Of course, He wanted her to protest, to say they needed to move the challenge, which he might be able to use, but she wasn't going to fall into that mistake. "Here will be fine, though I suggest folding the bench back in," she nodded to the one he had sat down on during his earlier visit.

"I'll get it done," he used the small control box to slide the bench back into the wall. "Anything else?"

"No, I believe that will be all." She moved to her feet, rolling out her shoulders before she picked up the mattress pad and set it against the wall. She had to deal with this the right way. If she didn't, he'd see a weakness he could use in the middle of the fight.

Too late to back out now.

She had too much wrapped up in this now. Not only pride but fear and a need to know who she was when she was with him. Perhaps losing was the answer.

No. I'm going to win.

He closed the door behind him, locking it before he turned his attention back to her. "Are you ready?"

Saying no wouldn't change things. It was time to get this over and done with. She couldn't think about failing either. If she did, she'd be entering into this fight as a loser. No, she had to handle this the way her father had taught her, with a clear mind. "I'm ready."

"To submission, as they say."

Corina nodded, watching him as she moved away from the walls, making sure there was plenty of room around her. She'd have to be careful. The close confines would make it too easy for the lack of space to be used against her. Then again, she could use the same lack against him. "Then, let's get this over and done with."

He moved before she had a chance to think about. Only pure instinct saved her from being taken down by the first move. She darted left, spinning on the ball of her right foot, catching him behind his right knee.

He growled, stumbling, but he recovered quickly. The small blow had given her enough time to put distance between them. Her heart raced, sweat beading across her brow as she tried to bring to focus on what she was doing. What he was doing.

"Slippy." He grinned, balancing his weight evenly. "I don't think you can stay out of my grasp long enough to make it count."

She bit back a response.

"Nothing to say?"

No, she wasn't going to waste her breath on exchanging words with him, when blows were the only answer. She simply smiled and took a step to the right, watching his eyes, searching for some sign he'd made a choice on his next move.

It didn't work. He didn't move.

Bugger.

Fine, he was careful. She couldn't blame him, not after the way the first move had failed. Where was his weakness? He had one, she knew he did, but finding it was another matter. Fuck, she was better than this.

David leaned forward, reaching for her right hand, but she kept the distance between them. Did he think she'd be that easy? "Why move away from me, Corina? You don't want to fight me, not really." His voice pitched low, purring, tempting as he held out his hand. "Come to me, and this can be over with."

Last Name

Was he insane? Corina bit her lip and didn't speak.

"You don't want to fight, why else would you refuse to make a real move against me?" He taunted, reaching out for her again with his left hand this time. "Admit it, Corina."

But she did want to fight. She needed to fight so she could, if she lost, still claim her status as a warrior. Yes, maybe being in his arms, being at his feet, would be fun to explore for a short time. Under the right circumstances. With the ability to say no at any time...

Stop thinking about it. This is what he wants me to do. He wants me distracted.

His fingers brushed against her right sleeve, and she had just enough warning to skip to the left and out of his reach before his hand closed on what was now empty air. Now he was pissing her off.

She growled, turned, one hand grasping the other, and slammed both clenched fists toward his shoulder as she completed the turn. Empty air greeted the blow, and she stumbled, barely getting her balance back before he made a move.

He was behind her before she was aware of it, one hand tangling in her hair, yanking and pulling her back, but her reaction time improved. She twisted under the grip, grimacing at the pain lanced across her scalp during the process, but once she faced him, the stress placed on his arm was enough to use. She slammed one hand up, connecting with the underside of his elbow, slamming it with every ounce of strength she had.

He cried out, letting go of her hair and shaking out his arm. "Nasty."

"So was the hair grip." She growled, her hands clenched into tight fists. Fine, he'd taunted her into replying. She had to get her emotions back under control. Ignore the comments, the tempting lines, and focus on fighting.

Focus on winning. This wasn't a game. This was life. Her life.

Her freedom. He ability to make choices and walk the path she wanted to walk instead of answering to him when she wanted to do something with her life.

"You have long hair, I'd be a fool not to use it in a fight, lover." He shook his arm again, but his face showed signs of the pain he was in. "And I'm many things in life but not a fool."

Had she struck hard enough to crack a bone? A weakened limb or spot on the body became a punch point in a fight.

"You've tried, but it's time to give up." He moved toward her, and they circled, small feints made by them both, testing for any weakness they could use. "Nowhere left for you to go, my girl. Except kneeling, at my feet. It's what you want to do, and we both know it."

Corina shook her head, her lips pressed into a tight, thin line, jaw clenched as she watched him. Where was the opening? Shit, he wasn't giving her one. Sweat beaded across her brow, her muscles aching as the dance continued. How long they tested each other with small movements, grabs, or quick steps, she had no way of knowing, but it could have been hours. Then it came. He reached for her with his damaged arm, and she struck.

Her left hand grasped and tightened around his wrist. Her right flew out, slamming into the damaged arm at the elbow, hitting full force before she twisted the arm. He cried out, arching his back, moving onto his toes but she was focused on the arm and didn't see the other blow coming.

Despite the pain he was in, he'd been able to bring his left hand around in a closed fist. A fist slammed into her ribs, knocking the wind from her. She gasped, letting go of his wrist, but she managed to grab it again tight through sheer determination.

"Let. Go. Of. Me." Each word accompanied by a new blow and by the fourth, she had no choice. She grunted, her hand releasing his wrist, and she tried to step back, needing to catch her breath.

He wasn't going to give her the time to recover.

She tried to scramble away but breathing hurt, and for a

moment, one dangerous moment, she stood, gasping for breath, one hand pressed over her now aching ribs. Had he cracked one?

Shit.

David moved in, closing the small distance between them, forcing her to stumble back until she hit the wall. She tried to slide to the left, but his hand shot out, grabbing her by the throat and he pinned her to the wall.

"It's. Over."

Chapter Fifteen

David met her gaze as he growled those two words at her. His heart raced, his cock hard under his pants, the need to take her down and take her down hard threatened to become all-consuming.

"No," she whispered, struggling against the wall. "It's not." Her hands moved, fingers grasping at his wrist. Short but still sharp nails dug into his skin as she fought to break free. "No, it can't be. It can't be over. I'm not ready to give up. Damn you, I'm not ready."

He tightened his grip on her throat. If he had to choke her out to win the fight, then that's exactly what he'd do. She had to submit, and he had to win, or he'd lose her once and for all. Not a risk he was willing to take. *Mine. She's mine.* "Submit."

She shook her head, twisting. The kick landed against his thigh instead of between his legs had been expected. This was, after all, a no holds barred fight. If she wanted to go for the family jewels, she was allowed. And he could press down on her throat and knock her out.

Corina gasped, struggling to breathe as his hold became relentless. A low whimper formed in the back of her throat, fear flashing in her beautiful eyes. "No, you can't do this. You know this isn't going to work. You have to let me go. David, please."

For a moment, he was tempted. Would it be so bad to let her go and forget about all of this?

Not. Happening.

"Yes, I can do this and I will unless you submit." His voice became cold, as cold as he knew himself to be inside. He'd never pushed a fight with her this far before. Never put her under threat of unconsciousness or death, and now she was faced with a side of him; she never believed existed in him.

The side willing to do whatever it took to win.

She kicked again, frantically this time. She lashed out with both feet as she smacked the underside of his arm, trying to loosen his grip.

"It's not going to work, love." He leaned in closer, his lips a breath from hers. "Submit, and it will all be over. Submit and accept you lost. Accept a part of you truly did want to lose before the fight began."

She bared her teeth in a snarl, but it was halfhearted at best. Doubt mingled with fear in her eyes, a soft tremble working through her body and her pulse rapid under his grip.

It was almost done. The fight in her eyes fading before she uttered the words.

"I-I submit." The words choked out, a sob barely swallowed before it gained life.

He nodded, once and let go of her throat, allowing her to slide down the wall before he took two steps back, giving her the space she'd need to come to terms with what had happened. She hadn't had a chance, not in a room this small. Perhaps it hadn't been fair to force the issue here, but he'd had to use what he had, and she didn't need to know the small mess hall doubled as a gym when needed, wasn't much bigger.

Besides, there'd have been witnesses to the fight if it had taken place elsewhere, and neither of them needed that. It would be hard enough for Corina to adapt to the changes as it was.

Corina rubbed the red mark on her throat, shuddering as she sat on the cool metal floor. Her hands shook, and she didn't look up at him. Small wisps of hair hung over her temple, sticking to the skin where beads of sweat had caught the strands, and David swallowed down the urge to help her to her feet.

"Do you need medical attention, Corina."

"No, Captain," she spoke softly, the tremble more obvious in her voice.

"No, sir." He insisted. "You lost the challenge, remember."

She flinched and nodded.

His heart sank. Shit, this wasn't going to be easy. She hated him now. She had to. She'd lost her freedom and had been told she would be submissive to him. A part of him wanted to snap at her, make her understand this had been her fault, her decision. Instead, he took a deep breath and offered her his good hand. She'd done a number on his arm, and he'd have to have it checked, but he could still help her up.

"Take my hand, please." He softened his tone, hoping she'd see it as a kindness not him trying to prove she was weak. Shit, she was far from soft. He'd be the first to admit it. But her heart, no matter what she might think, hadn't been in the fight. If it had, he'd have been hurt far worse than this. She wasn't a weakling when it came to conflicts or to life, but she needed to accept this part of the battle was over.

Corina slid her hand into his but still didn't lift her gaze as he helped her to his feet.

"Look at me," he kept his voice soft. He couldn't let her slide too far into despair. Besides, it wasn't going to be that bad. He'd find a way to help her find the balance even if it took the rest of his life.

"No, thank you, sir."

"It wasn't a request." He cupped her chin and lifted her face to see into her eyes. He could do this regardless of the part of him screaming in protest. *Get it under control. She's yours now. Don't blow it.* "Don't make this any harder than it has to be love. I won. But it doesn't change how I feel for you."

"How can it not change how you feel for me? I lost. I. Bloody. Lost." She snapped and drew away from his touch. "I have to bend to your wishes now no matter what they may be. Be submissive when it's - it's wrong. And not only in the bedroom. If you want, you can push me far enough that I lose all the respect I've built in my time amongst the peacekeepers. Collar and chains, yeah, I know how far this can go. And did I think about that before issuing the challenge?" She took a breath and fought to bring the trembles under control. "Fuck. Yes, but I assumed I'd win. Damn you, I believed I could win. I didn't want to lose. Not when it counted." Her voice trailed off as the first of the tears appeared in her eyes and glistening before they slipped down her cheeks.

He sighed and pulled her into his arms, wrapping them around her tightly. This was a reaction he hadn't expected. She wasn't the type to cry. Not normally. Damnit, he was supposed to protect her from pain, not inflict in on her. "It's not going to be like that. I'm not going to destroy you, Corina. It was never my plan. I want you to be happy, but I'm not fool enough to believe such comes without work from both of us." He whispered into her hair, rubbing her back with one hand. "You'll be submissive in the bedroom but not in life in general. It's all I'm going to ask for. As for work, I'm still trying to figure it out. But I won't destroy you. Doing that would be like destroying a part of myself."

She took a deep breath, the sobs silent as they wracked through her body. "I'm not a slave, it's not who I am. I'm a warrior and always will be."

"And I've always loved that about you. Before you took this path so seriously, you were still never one to back down. Nor will I ask you to now." He cupped the back of her head and tipped it up. "I love you, and you don't destroy the one you love." He leaned in and brushed his lips over hers.

She whimpered, trying to pull back.

"No, we're alone now. When we're alone, then I'll insist on the submission. When we're with others, that's when we can be equals." It wasn't the right way to say it, but it would do for now. "All right?"

Corina hesitated before she nodded her voice shaky when she did finally forced herself to speak. "I-I think I can live with that, sir."

"Good, because trust me, it's all I'm going to ask of you." He believed it, even if a small part of him wanted to drag her down into the darkness and push her to such depths of submission neither of them had ever experienced before. Yet it would be wrong.

Delicious, exciting, but wrong.

He'd accept what was realistic between them. Accept, embrace, and keep the woman he knew and loved in his life, without destroying the best part of her.

"I trust you... "

With those soft words, she'd taken the first step.

Corina closed her eyes as his lips claimed hers. Only in private, no public submission. Had he meant it? She didn't want to cling to a hope without knowing he meant it. But he'd said it, said he wasn't going to push things with her to a point where she'd break. He wasn't going to humiliate her, or force her into a situation which would destroy her if that meant letting the walls down when they were behind closed doors, she'd at least try.

It was all she could promise, and she knew it wasn't going to be easy.

It will be hard but not impossible. I can do this. I know I can do this.

"Focus on me, love. Turn your mind to what we're doing," he broke the kiss long enough to speak.

Then his hand tightened in her hair, fisting as he pulled her head back, tipping her chin up. His lips covered and dominated hers, parting them with a firm push of his tongue.

She groaned, shuddering against him. His tongue moved inside her mouth, conquering, stroking, his kiss hard, brutal and yet loving all at the same time. He stole her breath, his hand never easing as it moved through her hair, as his tongue explored and claimed her mouth, leaving her lips swollen and bruised.

He ended the kiss, staring down into her eyes. "Such beautiful lips, all pink, soft, and willing. I'm going to feel those on my cock, lover." He used the grip on her hair to ease her to her knees.

"Show me what you can do."

She tensed for a moment, uncertain about this. It wasn't as though she'd never given him oral before, but not like this. Not as a command, nor was she ready for the heat between her thighs. Her clit throbbed, needing his touch, or her own, and her inner walls clenched.

"Do it, love. Make me proud." He let go of her hair and smiled. "Show me your submission, your acceptance is real and not a means of putting me off until you can find a way to be free of me."

A way she knew would only come with death or his willing release of her. The first she knew she didn't want. The second – the idea of it knotted her guts.

Corina reached up and opened David's pants, freeing his cock. It was thick, long, and hard, rock hard, with a small bead of pre-come already forming on its glossy tip. She cupped his erection in both hands, stroking it slowly, letting herself become used to the feel of it as she settled her ass on her heels, trying to find a way to be comfortable.

Stop thinking of comfort and focus on this.

She closed her eyes and took a deep breath, steadying her nerves.

"Slow and easy. No rush remember?"

No one would disturb them in the cell unless there was an emergency. And while she could have been upset with this taking place in the cell, at least no one else had been able to see the state of her after the fight, nor guess what had happened. She opened her eyes and looked up at him as she moved her hands up and down the length of his cock, smiling when it twitched in her grasp. She reached down, cupping his balls with one hand before she closed her lips around the head of his shaft.

He shuddered at the first touch of her tongue to his soft skin, his hand reaching and touching her head, but not grasping her hair when she circled the head of his cock with her tongue before flicking it rapidly over the swollen skin.

"Fuck," he hissed and moved his hand away from her hair.

He wasn't going to use it to control her actions. That gave her more leeway and confidence to do what she knew was needed. She lowered her lips slowly down the length of his cock, working it with her hand as her free hand played with and massaged his balls. The taste of his arousal grew in her mouth, and she swallowed, once before she suckled on his shaft.

"Gods, yes." He thrust, deeply, into her mouth but didn't grasp for her head. "Fuck, you've not lost any skill, my girl."

Girl? She wasn't a girl anymore. She was a grown woman who deserved to be treated as such, yet the phrasing sent a ripple of pleasure through her body, centering on her throbbing clit. *But I am his, he's made it clear. I lost the fight. I have to deal with this, with all of this.*

She refocused on the task at hand, shutting out the random thoughts as best as she could. His cock filled her mouth, and she ran her tongue underneath the length of his cock.

He thrust slowly in and out of her mouth and she dropped her hand away from his sac, letting it slap, lightly, against her chin. With her lips and tongue at work he groaned, picking up the pace as he filled her mouth over and over again.

"Gods, I can't do this much longer. Not unless I want to take my pleasure only of your mouth." He pulled free of her lips and took a step back, shuddering in delight. "Hands and knees, Corina. Hands and knees, and butt in the air."

She paled at his words. Did he plan on using her ass again?

A part of her wanted him to do just that...

She eased back to her feet and let her gaze tracing the line of his body before she turned, slowly and moved back down to her hands and knees. She was still dressed, but he hadn't told her to strip down either. Right now, she had to focus on what he wanted.

A strand of hair fell across her eyes, and she tried to blow it out of the way.

She waited, her head lowered, her heart racing as she tried to keep herself in position.

"Arch your back a little more, Corina." His voice a soft, velvet whisper behind her. "And part your thighs."

She did as he ordered, and took a deep breath, trying to keep her panic from growing any more. She had to do this. Her fingers clenched, but the metal floor offered nothing for her to grip. No purchase for her short nails as she remained in position.

David reached down and touched her in the small of her back. His touch firm but gentle as he brushed down over the swell of her backside. "You're beautiful, Corina. More than you've ever been willing to accept, and I won't push you in public. I won't embarrass you. This submission, the beauty of it all, will be between us. You have my word."

With a soft whimper, she leaned into his touch, enjoying the pass of his hand over her still covered buttocks. Was he going to undress her, or did he want to test her? She didn't care right now, and she wanted to enjoy it. Wanted to lean into his touch and relax. She could trust him. She had to trust him, or this would never work.

"Are you ready for this?" He asked and lifted his hand, slapping it back down against her backside with a sharp crack.

She gasped, her hips jerking under the blow. Pain and heat combined to then filter between her thighs. She lowered her head, trying to hold the position, but it wasn't easy.

"Well?" A second blow landed with a louder crack.

She gasped, jerking again. She tried not to press her thighs together, but the heat was growing with each passing moment. "I-I don't know, sir."

"Yes, you do." A third blow landed, and she cried out. Each one was harder than the one before. "Are you ready for this? Are you ready to be mine once and for all?"

I am his, what is he talking about?

Three more hard fast spanks struck, and she sobbed, arching with the blows. "Sir, please. Please."

"Please what, Corina?" He purred the word as he settled on his knees behind her. "Tell me what you want, Corina. Tell me what you want from me. Tell me you belong to me." He reached for the fastening on her pants and tugged them down around her thighs along with her panties. "I want to hear it from your own lips, my girl."

She tensed as he pulled them down, flushing with hunger and embarrassment. She couldn't say. It wasn't in her nature to be this vocal, not like this at least. She caught her bottom lip between her teeth and whimpered, "I can't, sir."

"Can't or won't?" He reached up, grasping her by the hair. "You have to answer me, Corina. You don't get a choice in this anymore." His grip tightened as he tangled her hair and tugged on it, forcing her head up and back. "You have to give me what I want in private."

Won't. Can't.

"Corina, obey me."

She understood what was expected of her, but doing it was another matter entirely. She whimpered, her back tight, head forced back, the words on her lips but locked inside her mouth.

Say it. All you have to do is say it, and he'll relent. It's not that hard. But it was. *You have the strength.*

"Sir, please. I-I want to be yours. I need to be yours. Y-you won the challenge, I belong to you from this point onward."

He growled in delight and pressed his cock between her thighs. With one harsh thrust, he filled her, stretching her inner walls until she sobbed in pleasure and arched back into him.

"Yours. I'm yours." She gasped, rocking with him.

His balls slapped against her swollen nether lips, the sound echoing through the room, mingling with their shared cries and grunts. Pressure built within, the friction delicious with each deep thrust into her body. Her pants, still halfway down her thighs, forced her legs together, adding to the pressure and pleasure rolled through her system.

He yanked on her hair, sending small shards of pain lancing across her scalp, and she cried out, trying to shake her head free, but she couldn't. Not with how he held her. How he controlled her.

David pulled back until only the head of his cock rested within her body, forcing her to wait, to slow down for a moment. His breath, ragged and loud behind her, rang in her ears.

"Sir?" She whimpered, wanting to see him, but he hadn't let go of her hair.

"Wait, girl, breathe, and give your body a moment before you continue."

But she didn't want to give it a moment. She wanted him now. Needed him now. "Please."

"Impatient aren't you?" He chuckled and slapped her ass with his free hand. "Rotate your hips for me."

She groaned but did as he ordered, tipping her hips, rotating slowly on his cock but he still didn't move. She tried to press back, but he slapped her backside again, sharply this time.

"No moving back. Rotate, work those muscles for me. Let me enjoy what I own now."

Own. The word made her want to growl and sob at the same time. His. She was his. She had the capability to dance for him, move for him. That came not from her father's training, but her mothers. The slow, sensual dance which was very much a part of the Gaean pleasure adept. She'd been young, damned young, when her mother had originally taught her the moves.

Now she would put those moves to their true use.

Corina tipped her pelvis, tightening and releasing on her inner walls as she circled on his erect cock, feeling each inch of his penis inside her. Feeling it and using it. She focused, rippling the muscles of her abdomen, shimmying on him before she circled first to the left then to the right, alternating in time to the pace set by her own need.

"Yes." He cried out beneath her.

She lifted until only the tip of his cock remained within her body and her inner walls clenched on the sensitive spot causing him to groan in delight. "Yes, again, Corina. That's it, you're doing it."

For a moment, his voice drew her out of what she was doing, her own pleasure threatening to take control until she focused once more trying to get her body to tighten around him once more. She could do this. She had him close to the edge. All she had to do was keep her body under control.

"You don't know how much I've missed the feel of your body against mine, my love," he growled in delight, thrusting into her body with one, deep, harsh stroke. "Fuck, this is what I've needed. This is what we both needed."

She couldn't argue, she belonged with him. Her body and mind both knew and accepted it. She whimpered, closing her eyes, and met his thrusts. Her inner walls clenched, relaxed and gripped again on the hard, thick length of his cock. She was damn close now, and her body shuddered with the need to come.

Pain and pleasure combined. The pressure building to the point where she might explode. Too much. This was too much.

"Keep going, my girl. Don't stop now."

Obey. She had to obey him. Her hips rolled with his thrusts, "please sir... I can't hold any longer."

"Then don't," he lifted his free hand and smacked down against her bare backside with a loud crack.

She cried out, her hips jerking, a sob of pain and pleasure escaped. Her body clenched in delight, her inner walls rippling along the length of his cock. Joy surged through her, building in her body, threatening to rip the sanity from her soul. She'd never experienced this before. Never known the strength of the submission he'd torn from her.

Won from her.

"Come for me, Corina. Come for me now."

Her body obeyed, and she cried out. She sobbed, bucking

under him, her hips rolling and pressing back against him. She twisted, needing more, needing less, needing this to end before she tumbled into the depths of insanity.

"I love you, David. I've always loved you." She cried out as she collapsed beneath him.

He thrust one last time and fell on top of her. "I'm never going to let you go, Corina. I love you too much to go through that again."

Chapter Sixteen

"You're doing what?" The strange male voice snapped Corina awake. "I need you to repeat that because I don't think you heard you correctly."

"I'm handing in my resignation, sir. I don't know how else to phrase it to make things clear to you."

David? She frowned and blinked the sleep from her eyes. Yes, it had to be David but who was he talking to? She turned her head, slowly, toward the sound of the two voices. Handing in his resignation? She was missing a detail here? She tried to focus on the conversation.

Where the hell am I?

Not the cell. Of course, David had moved them to his quarters after the fight and claiming. They'd only run into one member of the crew on the way, but they'd been able to avoid any conversation. Nothing more than an exchange of nods.

But it didn't explain who David was talking to.

"Over what? The female?" The new speaker growled. "How can you think of walking away? And for a relationship you don't even know will work. I expected better from you, Monroe. You have a real future with the Rangers, and you plan on giving all of it up for a quick, fucking, screw."

That female? Whoever spoke had made one big. Fucking. Mistake.

"No, not over a female. I'm handing in my resignation over my wife. I've spent long enough searching for the right one, and now I've claimed her I'm not going to give up on her. If I stayed with the service you'd find a way to pull us apart." David spoke calmly despite the anger in the other man's voice. "It's why I have to do this."

Corina sat up and rolled out her shoulders as she watched David. He was sat in front of a desk, speaking to a holographic image of a man. A man in a uniform she didn't recognize. Her heart raced as she let the conversation process slowly through her mind. Was he doing this? Giving up his career? She took a deep breath and tried – but failed – to keep her voice calm.

Would she be able to do the same thing? Walk away from duty, from the world she had built for herself, to spend the rest of her life with him?

I already did.

By losing the challenge, she'd placed her life, her career, entirely in his hands.

"What the hell is going on?" She forced her voice to remain calm.

"I'm handing in my resignation so I can be with you, Corina."

"Like hell you will," the other male protested. "I won't accept your resignation. You're a vital part of my team, and I don't have to accept your papers, Monroe."

"And how are you going to force him to stay?" Corina moved to her feet, wrapping the sheet around her body. The last thing she wanted was to flash the stranger, and she had no idea how much the man could see. Hell, she didn't know what work he was involved in. She took a deep breath and forced herself to keep calm. "Are you going to chain him to a desk? Amusing. I might enjoy watching him be confined, but I don't think it's going to do you any good."

"Monroe, what the fuck is she doing in here?" The holographic image flickered. "You didn't warn me she was in the damned room."

"Considering I finalized things between us I'll leave it to your imagination what we were doing and what she's doing here," David replied, calmly. "She has a point, however. How do you expect to force me to stay in service, sir? All I have to do is turn this ship around and return to the station, and there's nothing you can do except issue a kill order on me. Are you prepared to do that?"

Shadow Rangers, of course. The information came flooding back as she moved to her feet and walked over to the desk, her gaze never moving from the flickering holographic figure. "And if you do place a kill order on him, you'll have to get through me. Not only me but my clan."

"And I'd care about your threat why? You're one woman. One lone peacekeeper. You've no idea the force I can bring to bear if I want to." The man shook his head, his tone cool and mocking. "You're no threat to me."

"You're a fool," she spoke softly.

The middle-aged man shook his head again. "Do you think you can scare me this easily, Corina Greenheart?"

Why is it men find it easy to dismiss a woman's desire to protect her own? No matter if they know better than to pull this shit? "If it isn't enough to make you think twice, then think about this." She leaned in close, one hand holding onto the sheet. "Never piss off a mated warrior because I swear by Mars and Gaea if you harm him, I'll hunt you to the ends of the universe even if it takes my last breath to bring you down if you kill my mate. There will be nothing in this universe which will be able to protect you. Nowhere you can run that I won't be able to find you. So back the fuck off. Unless you want one pissed off bitch tracking you down?"

"This one has steel." For a moment, there was nothing but silence in the small room. When the flickering hologram finally responded the man's tone had changed to one of begrudging respect. "Perhaps you've made the right choice after all, Monroe."

"Yes, sir. I've made exactly the right choice. Do you accept my resignation?" David Monroe glanced at Corina before he continued. "I can have my official papers in the moment you tell me your decision."

"Fine. I don't like it, but resignation accepted. Get the work sent in then return to *Freedom Station*. I'll have to arrange for another to take Captaincy of your ship." The man, or rather the holographic version of him, turned his attention to Corina. "You'd have been an interesting woman to work with, Greenheart. Should you ever want a change in career, talk to Monroe here, and we'll arrange a meeting."

It was never going to happen, not after what she'd found out about the Shadow Rangers. The way they'd treated David for and whatever they'd been involved in on the station were enough to send her running in the opposite direction. "Thank you for the offer, but I suggest you refrain from holding your breath on that one."

"One can hope," the image flickered and vanished from David's desk.

Corina sighed relief washing through her body. It was over. She turned and stared at David, the realization of exactly what he'd done hit her full force. "You did that, for me? You turned your back on your career and your friends, for me? I don't understand. Why would you do it? You won the challenge, you're in charge, you have the right to tell me to quit my post and walk away from my career."

David moved to her side and cupped her cheek. "Because it was and still is the right thing to do."

She leaned into his touch, not understanding at first. "He could have ordered you killed, you must have known that before he told you, and yet you still did it." She swallowed hard, trying to keep her emotions under control. No one had ever made such a sacrifice for her before now. Yet he had. This man who had left her three years ago had now sacrificed it all to be with her, and no going back now.

"I know." David's thumb moved slowly over her cheek, his voice tender.

"Why? And please, don't tell me it was the right thing to do, there's more to this. Has to be." She shook her head and pulled away from his hand, meeting his gaze before she spoke again. "You didn't have to do this for me, David. You had the power, and you gave it up, for me."

David pulled her against his chest and wrapped his arms around her. "No, you don't understand Corina. I haven't given up the power, I've chosen how to use it. If I'd made you leave the station, the Peacekeepers, then I'd have been forcing you into a truly uncomfortable position to do what? Continue on working with the Shadow Rangers when I'd stopped being truly happy working for them three years ago."

"Three years..." when he'd walked out on her, "I didn't know."

"Your job was the only thing I had left to give you, love." He cupped her chin and brushed her lips with his.

Corina shivered, her eyes half closing. "No, there's one other thing you can give me."

"And that is?"

Corina reached up, encircling his neck with her hands, her lips a breath away from his. "A last name; your last name."

His kiss was the only answer she needed.

If you enjoyed this story and would like to know more, please keep reading...

About the Author

Originally from England, Terri now lives in Minnesota with her husband, one child still at home, her pack sister, business partner, two service dogs and a host if imaginary voices. Her work ranges from the mild to the wild, and in 2019 Terri launched a second pen name, T.S. Weaver in order to writer her 'none smexy books'.

Please follow Terri via https://www.facebook.com/worldsofterripray/ and https://twitter.com/TerriPray_UTM

If you're interested in System Wars, her T.S. Weaver science fiction series, please consider joining https://www.facebook.com/groups/TSWeaverSystemWars/ where readers will gain sneak peeks of coming books, RPG information, artwork and the world building behind the System Wars setting.